Hindler's Lisp

By Jug Brown

To Cary & Tamara
Please enjoy this
one-
It's funny —
love, Andy.

4/16

ISBN 978-1-329-98506-3

I would like to thank Rik Huhtanen and Andrew Levine for their inspiration and assistance during the writing of this book. I have enjoyed every moment I spent with these two sterling creative forces. I look forward to seeing them again soon when we can once again share. Special thanks to Kim Torgerson for her support and Stewart Thomas for the cover illustration.

Chapter 1

On the night of his execution, Leo Laum volunteered at the local theater. His sins were plentiful. His snarky frat boy practical jokes flowed from him like waste from a leaky sewer. His trust fund ease of living rendered him entitled and unaccountable, until much later that evening.

The street lights were long bluish streaks on the wet black road. No traffic, still, empty. The bar workers had mostly straggled home and the bars were shut. It was quiet, damp and cool: an ordinary night in April in Eugene, Oregon.

The Hunter, parked in a deep shadow, window rolled down, sniffed the air. It was fresh. He could smell the fir trees that stood on the butte beside the train tracks nearby. A fine mist fell.

A bicyclist rode by in the dark, his helmet light flashing. The Hunter perked up, squinted to see the rider, and shook his head: it's not him.

He closed the window and focused once more on his laptop. He sighed, hoping for a breakthrough with his manuscript. He was so close to tying it all together. Hopelessly blocked for a long time, he was far from creating coherence. His confidence diminished each day. Month after month, he stared at the same pages. He was deeply depressed, yet stubbornly hanging on. His self-loathing became an unending negative energy source. He was paralyzed. He knew his once promising work was terrible. No matter how good the concepts were, the book was superficial and shallow. He had no idea how to make it work, how to end it, or how to stop himself from obsessing about it. His promising start had become a tormenting strait-jacket.

Sitting in the car in the night mist, the blackness and emptiness of the night mimicked his mood. Yet the fresh air gave him hope.

I can do this!

He concentrated, scrolling through the pages. With each page, he felt worse.

Then he saw the blood. It started pouring down the laptop screen. He closed his eyes and shook his head vigorously. The bloody vision always shook him up. The blood took him deep into his memory. When he opened his eyes, the blood was gone.

He took a deep breath and went back to scanning his pages.

What am I going to do with this mess?

He was looking at the screen when the bicyclist passed. He looked up and saw a bulky young man pedaling slowly past him across the street.

"Right on time, right on time," the Hunter sang to himself as he started his car. The motor came quietly to life.

"Man on a bike, man on a bike, man on a bike," he sang, and his heart pounded.

He pulled onto the street, kept his lights off. The lumbering bike was almost a half block away.

"Got you in my sights, got you in my sights Leo." He accelerated the car smoothly.

"Bike, bike, bike, bike." He chanted breathily.

The Hunter came up fast from behind until he was alongside Leo. He stamped on his brakes and hit Leo's right leg. He orchestrated the sudden stop to act like a chopping punch. Leo was hit hard and propelled into the side of a parked van. His helmet-less head popped as it smacked against the door panel. The blood streaked down the van, and he flopped in a heap beside it.

The Hunter breathed a sigh of release. He looked in his rear view. He could see the legs splayed in the shiny black street, the bike wheel bent and the handle bars turned completely around. The bike was still between Leo's legs.

The Hunter was ecstatic, trembling. His gloved hands gripped the wheel. He needed to make sure. He turned his lights on for the first time. His rear taillights made the body glow red.

Without warning, the vision of blood returned. He closed his eyes and stopped the car.

No, not now!

He returned instantly to the event that changed his life forever: the time he saw the blood for real. Images flooded in as he fought to gain control: the mobile hanging above the little bed, the muffled scream, wandering out into the kitchen, the blood; running from the person on the floor, who thrashed with horrible, blood-gurgling breathing. His little pajama feet wet with blood. The bloody hand, reached for his, and then went limp. He revisited the scene. How long had he sat there? Hours? All day? It felt so long. Strange arms lifted him up, the smell of stale tobacco and rough whiskers. "Call me Daddy."

The hunter opened his eyes. The dream of blood had disappeared. He snuffled his breath in and out, still trembling.

Did the bike man twitch? Did the leg move? He checked the rear view and examined the street with vigilant eyes. With the car in reverse, he aimed his tire at the man's head and there was an awful crunch. The Hunter let out a sigh.

It's done.

He accelerated forward and reveled in his relief. The solution to his manuscript problem appeared suddenly and clearly. The seamless web of connections in the storyline had completed itself. It was all there: the beginning, the middle, and the profound brilliant conclusion. The crushing paralysis was gone. He was excited to start writing. He took a deep calming breath.

Slow down. It'll keep.

It started to rain hard, a downpour that might last all night. The Hunter slowly drove across town and pulled into the all night car wash. Careful to keep his gloves on, he put in his quarters and pressure-washed the car thoroughly. He took a toothbrush out of his coat pocket and washed the tires and grill with bleach. He watched with satisfaction as the gore slid down the industrial slatted drain. When he was certain it was clean, he wiped the tires and grill with a towel. He threw away the towel, the bleach bottle and the toothbrush.

Now I'm ready to write.

He pulled out onto the street without stopping to check for traffic. He thought only of getting back to his desk to write.

The flashing lights of a police car lit up his rear view mirror. It jarred him. The cop was tailgating him, the siren gave a whoop.

I'm finished. It's over.

An image flooded in: he was wearing a baggy prison jumpsuit, in a cell on death row; a needle would be in his arm after years of boredom and waiting. He slowed down, and put on his turn signal.

They've got me.

He could barely breathe. The cop car passed him with a roar. The Hunter let out his breath as the patrol car accelerated down the road.

They probably found the man on a bike.

The Hunter felt overjoyed, incredibly alert and aroused by his victory. He drove carefully and put the car where he found it. He returned the keys where they belonged. No one would ever suspect.

He rushed to his desk, opened the laptop and started writing. The words and ideas flew out of him. He knew it was good, better than good, a masterpiece, a magnum opus.

At 4 a.m. his outline was finished. He was inspired. He knew he would stay productive for weeks, months. He went to bed. When he closed his eyes, he saw the twisted bike and the man's body on the wet, street. He felt wonderful. At 8:30 he awoke refreshed and walked out to greet the day.

Chapter 2

Some Time Earlier

Something always seems to go wrong before opening night in small town theater, and it happened with the play, *Family Table*. It all started on a late night in December, when, sitting alone in his dark office with papers flung everywhere, Eamon Krieg desperately wrote a $100,000 grant proposal to a foundation supporting and promoting new plays and new playwrights, a Hail Mary pass to save the Eugene Experimental Theater.

He heard about the grant only 6 hours before the deadline. It was from a prestigious New York City art foundation. It was longer than a long shot. Who was he to compete for a New York City arts grant?

But Eamon had some inside information. His sister, who ran an art gallery in Greenwich Village, knew the fund had extra money at the end of the year and needed to spend it. On December 30, she told Eamon about it. Eamon went to work immediately. Chugging espresso and Red Bull, Eamon, pulling at his beard and scratching his balding head, packed his grant proposal with bullshit and hope. He centered the proposal on the only new play available, *Family Table*. He submitted the grant just before the deadline and days later got the news: he won the grant.

Eamon felt this change of luck would transform the struggling Eugene Experimental Theater. He was no stranger to the ups and downs of small town theater; despite good reviews and enthusiastic volunteers, the red ink piled up, and they were weeks away from closing for good. The grant award was a lifesaver.

The grant came with a proviso: 5% of the money arrived with the award letter, the balance would be paid only if the play, *Family Table,* by Anonymous, was produced within the current

7

quarter of the year, and that four performances were given on a normal schedule.

Eamon's euphoria disappeared when he read this. He groaned.

Oh no, Family Table.

Family Table, by Anonymous, had sat in his bottom drawer, forgotten and unloved for a long time, perhaps years. It had arrived unsigned. A few people had taken the manuscript out to peruse it. Few had ever read the play to the end.

It was awful. No, it was worse than awful. It was offensive and insensitive. It was a compilation of caterwauling, inflammatory, and self-indulgent emotional accusations. All delivered in stylized psychobabble. If it had a redeeming aspect, it had to do with how shouting can sometimes make a person feel better: catharsis at all cost is the key to a better life. But getting to the end of the play was the challenge. Who could stay seated throughout the time it took to finish?

Certainly he tried to get a better play in those last few hours before the deadline. He searched for something decent to build his grant around. Hurried phone calls to theater people around the State failed to produce a viable option. One company in Ashland had a play, an award-winning student play called *The Saturday Club,* but they insisted on 50% of the grant money. Nobody was getting Eamon's money. No way. He and his theater had suffered in poverty for years, and with the money this close, even with the atrocious *Family Table,* Eamon wanted it all.

He deserved it. His theater had a great reputation for high-quality productions, but consistent funding had always eluded him. He had babied his theater through a decade of lean years and bill collectors, and he was now close to achieving the ultimate small town theater dream: stable funding, paid-up utilities, and a chance to reimburse past expenses to himself and others.

He had slammed the phone down.

No Ashland theater was getting a nickel of the grant money.

On that night in December, when all plan B's for Eugene Experimental Theater had been used up, when Eamon and his theater were at the end of the line, his luck had turned around. He was determined to give the play a successful run. He had a

Rolodex full of good contacts in the community, some advance money to keep the lights on, and only a simple set to build. All he needed was a stellar cast of local actors, to interpret and carry the play through four performances in April.

However, he did have trouble finding actors. He easily found student actors to play the two brothers and the sister, but nobody wanted to play the parents. He went through the Eugene A-List, the B-List, and finally badgered two local outcast actors with prickly reputations to play the loathsome Bernie and the treacherous Esther.

After finding his actors, the rest was easy. Eamon's sense of euphoria and destiny returned. To maintain control of the play, he decided to both produce and direct.

Four performances were all he needed to get the money. He explained the terms of the grant to the cast and crew, and with this shared vision in mind, they moved forward. Eamon was delighted that the grant didn't stipulate the public and the local reviewers liked the play. He was determined to get the money after four mandatory performances.

Let them hate it! Let them boo! Walk out! I don't care! I'll cry all the way to the bank!

Chapter 3

Family Table came together imperfectly. On opening night, with a full house, including the chairman of the grant fund, the wheels came off.

It all began with a fart, not just one fart, but a whole smelly series of them, trumpeted loudly by the actor, Reginald Holts, faithfully following the stage directions written in the play: "Bernie (the Father) must accompany his lines and interactions with loud, copious and effusive flatulence!"

Eamon Krieg had told Reginald Holt to ignore this specific stage instruction, but Reginald appeared on opening night full of method acting fervor, fully dressed, and in bloated, gaseous character. He was Bernie. He had embraced the part, learned his lines by heart, lived for weeks as Bernie, saturated himself in all things Bernie, including dietary predilections, and showed up just the way the part was written.

From his position off stage, Eamon groaned during the first fart, hoping it was the last. The audience even laughed a bit when Bernie, standing at the head of the table, wearing a birthday hat, said:

"Ahhh, now that was a good one! Maybe if you learned to cook, Mother, I would have a little better digestion."

"RRRRRRRRIIIIIIIIIIIIIIPPPPPPPPPPPPPPPP"

Esther takes off her party hat: "You eat like a pig. You always have. I married the wrong brother. Look at Norman. He's successful in business, handsome, a real man. And he has excellent manners. All of you should be ashamed, all except my lovely Richie, of course. You have the best manners dear."

Michael (son): "I eat slowly. I always have, Mother."

Gloria (sister): "Oh, right."

Esther (mom): "Stop calling attention to yourself, Michael. It's embarrassing. It makes you look insecure. With your weak chin and receding hairline, you can't afford it. You should learn from your brother."

Michael: "I have most of my hair."

Richie (brother, son) smiles and sits back in his chair: "Mr. Baldy, coming soon."

Esther (pointing at Bernie): "If you were more of a man—"

Bernie thunders: "Stop it this instant! Michael, Gloria, stop it."

They all stop.

Bernie: "We are here to celebrate your brother Saul's birthday, our little stillborn baby, a boy who would have been Richie's little brother."

Esther starts wailing. "My poor baby. Richie could have had a little brother. It's so sad."

Bernie, crying: "Richie could have taught him baseball. He would have been handsome, just like Richie. They would have been best friends."

RRRRRRRRRRRRRRRIIIIIIIIIIIIIIIIIIIIIPPPPPPPPPPPPPP. Another fart is loudly released.

Gloria: "He could have been my little brother, too."

Richie: "Ha. Oh please. The only thing you could have taught him is how to be a slut. Is that what you would have wanted for our little Saul, to be a slut?"

Michael: "I always loved baseball, Richie, and you hated it. I could have played catch with Saul."

Bernie, ripped another loud fart. "You are pathetic, Michael. Don't try to be an ass kisser. What could you have taught Saul? I am almost glad he didn't live to hear this conversation, or to be taught anything by either you or Gloria."

Esther, furious: "You wish . . . your own son . . . was never born? You worm!"

Bernie: "The only worm you are interested in is in the pants of other men! You're a slut."

Esther, turning on Gloria: "And you, why can't you find a nice Jewish boy to marry, instead of sleeping with every Tom, Dick and Harry goyim."

Bernie, joining in: "Yeah, what's wrong with you? Are you ashamed of your heritage? People died for your freedom."

RRRRRRRRIIIIIIIIIIIIIIIIIIIPPPPPPPPPPPPPPP

The stage smelled like a poorly ventilated bathroom.

Michael: "I married a nice Jewish girl."

Gloria: "Oh please, Michael. And she left you after two years."

Esther: "And no grandchildren. How could you do that to me?"

Michael: "It was simple irreconcilable differences. We grew apart. We're still friends to this day."

Esther: "Nah. You're like your father. You can't satisfy a woman. Not like my Richie. He can have any woman he likes. You're the best."

Gloria: "None of Richie's girls are Jewish! Why can't you see that?"

Bernie: "There, there, Gloria. Don't you see? It doesn't matter. I'm sure that whatever nice girl Richie chooses to marry will convert to Judaism. Then the children will be Jewish." He spreads his arms. "No problem, see? How come you're so dense? Now let's cut the cake."

Esther: "If you were a better provider, we could afford a better cake."

RRRRRRRRRRRRRIIIIIIIIPPPPPPP. The smell was starting to become unbearable.

"Another prize winner, eh kids?"

The fart smell had moved like a fog into the theater

Eamon noticed people nervously shifting in their seats. A few had already walked out. The chairwoman from the art grant foundation was still out there, in the front row. Eamon caught her looking toward the back rows.

I bet she'll move back farther after the intermission. Eamon guessed. *Maybe everyone will leave, but who cares?*

He walked to the back door of the theater, opened it, and stood outside in the rainy night, feeling pretty darn good, and getting a deep lungful of fresh air. The cast and crew will no doubt need a little propping up, to keep them motivated. He started composing his pep talk.

Only three more nights of this and we'll have all the money we need.

Chapter 4

The disintegration of *Family Table* continued during the cast and crew meeting after opening night. Even though it was cold and raining outside, Eamon opened the doors and turned on the exhaust fan to high. Reginald's profound farting had filled the whole theater. The cast and crew shivered in jackets on the set, anxious to get home.

"All right folks, pretty good night, don't you think? Full house tonight! I appreciate all of your efforts. Three more performances next weekend and this theater will be well funded. Then we can do many of the projects that you have suggested. This is a monumental achievement for our little theater. Keep up the good work, and thank you all."

RRRRIIIIPPPP!!!

Leo Laum, a volunteer technician, sitting in the back, burst out laughing: "Hey, time to get out of character, Reggie, don't you think?"

Audrey Sells, who played Esther, looked unhappy. "Oh, do you really think that was necessary? Eamon said you didn't have to follow the script on the farting bit. For goodness sake, please."

Reginald stood from the table and adjusted the silk scarf draped over his camel hair sport coat.

"I," he began imperiously, "am a professional, unlike you, and you and you. I live the part. I become the man. I studied in Los Angeles. I become the play. In fact, I carry this play on my shoulders. My film credits include parts in twenty movies. Have you any credibility whatsoever to question me?"

"I played summer stock theater in the Catskills one summer" she replied defensively.

"Ha!"

Eamon saw trouble and tried to head it off.

"Let's all agree to leave the farting out next week, ok?" He looked at Reginald. "Can we just agree to that?"

13

Reginald stared at Eamon with a haughty look.

"What movies were you in?" shouted Leo Laum with juvenile glee, not willing to let it go. "Were you in Fart Wars? Fart Trek? Fart by Fartwest? Fartigo?"

Audrey Sells and a few others chuckled mildly. Reginald turned red. Most of the cast and crew looked downward. They were tired and a little embarrassed.

"Enough of that," said Eamon. "Just a little kidding among friends, blowing off steam and all that, but that's enough for now alright? We are all on the same team. We have three more performances to go and then we are done with this stinking play, right?" The group chuckled.

"Sir Reginald has nearly blown the roof off this performance," said Leo.

"Okay, Leo, that's enough," said Eamon sharply.

Leo ignored him and continued with obnoxious, sophomoric fart jokes. "He played the wind in 'Goon with the Wind.'" No one laughed.

Audrey stood up and faced Reginald. "You are a gasbag, a wind bag, a dirty old fraud that nobody can stand. How dare you call yourself a professional? If you are so wanted, why aren't you in LA? What are you doing here? I'll tell you. Nobody will work with you."

"I have an agent . . . outrageous, you . . . small-minded, no-talent! I played with Richard Chamberlain once."

She shook her head. "What did you play? A dead body? Second man in the third row of a crowded train. Fraud," said Audrey.

"Please everyone. Let's calm down." Eamon asserted.

"I hear he filled the Goodyear blimp for the Super Bowl," said Leo.

Several people laughed.

"Enough! I quit! Your loss." shouted Reginald, turning away, and moving toward the door.

"Please, Reginald," said Eamon.

At the door, he stopped. "By the way, this one is for all of you . . ."

RRRRRRRRRRRRRRIIIIIIIIIIIIIIIIIIIIIIIIIPPPPPPPPPPPPPPP.

"Oh good, he's going," said Leo. "We can finally close the door. It's freezing in here."

The cast sat in stunned silence.

"Leo," said Eamon. "Did you really have to goad him like that?"

Leo shrugged. "I saw an opportunity. I took it. How often do you get a chance like that?"

"Who's going to play Bernie?" asked Audrey. "There are no understudies."

Eamon scratched his balding head. He stroked his beard. He rubbed his ample belly. He was a tallish man, thin legs, narrow chest and shoulders, scrawny neck, yet full in the belly.

"I'll play Bernie."

"Do you know the lines?" Audrey asked.

"I will learn them. We will add a book to the table props. I will appear intent on reading from time to time. We'll get through it."

Audrey wasn't convinced. "Unbelievable. What a disaster. Let's call the whole thing off."

"No no no no. We can't do that. We have three more shows to do, and then it's over. It will be okay, Audrey." Eamon assured her.

"I am a professional too, for your information."

"Of course you are Audrey. You're a wonderful performer. I have loved and admired your work for years."

Eamon looked around at the faces. Most of the crew and cast had not participated in the meeting. Many were looking down at their laps, tired, or up at the ceiling, bored. Eamon wondered how many would be back for the next performance.

Audrey exhaled a big breath. "You are as big a gasbag as Reginald. Worse."

"We have a few days off. Meet here on Friday at 3 p.m. for a run through before the next show. I have to go meet the Chairwoman of the grant foundation for drinks. Could I get a volunteer to clean up the snack area, sweep the stage and close everything up?"

Leo raised his hand.

"Thank you. See you all on Friday."

15

"You better learn your lines," warned Audrey.

The crew filed out into the dark and stood at the back door of the theater.

"We're going for a drink. We gotta air out after all that."

"I'll catch up with you when I'm done here," shouted Leo.

They walked ahead. After a quick sweep, Leo caught up with them on his bike. After a night of shots and beer and idiocy, they all left for home. Leo, a bit tipsy, unlocked his bike and made his way out onto the wet dark street.

Within minutes he was dead.

Chapter 5

Just a few days after Leo's death, the curtain rose for the second night of *Family Table*. The production was in immediate danger. The theater was less than half full. Two crew members including the ticket taker failed to show up. Eamon, in full costume and greasepaint for his part as Bernie, sold tickets.

Even the nicest of the Eugene theater reviewers had scorched the play. One reviewer said, "For the sake of all humanity and all that is merciful, stop the misery, pull the plug." Eamon expected it. The money was still his with the completion of three more performances.

Facebook "friends" from inside and outside the cast and crew, called for the play to be cancelled. Fortunately for Eamon Krieg, a few face-planted friends demanded that "the show must go on."

All week Eamon cajoled all involved to keep the play moving ahead. The need to complete four performances was his priority. Eamon put out fires, and put an urgent yearning tactic to work: Do it for "our Leo," our "fallen one." Eamon's sincere and tearful condolences could have been accompanied by a violin as he went from one player to the next to illicit participation.

Poor Leo, a life snuffed out too soon, a tender soul missed by all.

Hat in hand he recited his regrets over the tearful loss of the "genius" that had been in their midst, Leo. He shook his head and looked at his feet. A more somber and conciliatory presence could not have been conceived.

Eamon never learned Bernie's lines, not a single one.

In fact, he never got a chance to open the script.

He ran from the ticket booth to the set when the lights went down. He stumbled to his place on the set, overturning a chair in the process. He had hidden his script in several places on the set. He wanted to be able to look slightly downward and recite the lines that stood on the open page.

Someone had taken Eamon's bookmark out of the script, and he had forgotten his reading glasses. Audrey Sells, playing Esther, scowled and shook her head, as he found his glasses in his coat pocket, found the page, and discovered that the reason no one was speaking was because the first line in the play was his.

Bernie: "What a terrible day I had! I tell you, there's never been a bigger horse's ass than that pipsqueak son of the owner. Kid doesn't know anything. And he's my boss?"

He looked up. Audrey had the next line. She was staring at Eamon with revulsion and a vicious, thin smile that told Eamon and anyone else: hating you is perfectly in character, so I think I'll enjoy it.

Esther: "If you weren't such a failure, maybe you could have been the boss. How long have you been there? Twenty-five years? And what have you made of yourself in that time? You're still doing the same job."

Eamon looked down at the script and continued.

Bernie: "Wait a minute. UNFAIR! You sit here all day eating food that I put on the table, and when I come home, all I want is some respect. You . . . "

Gloria: "Remember how sad it was around here when I had to rent a prom dress and couldn't buy one. That was horrible of you, Daddy. All the other girls had new dresses."

Richie: "That's nothing. Remember when I had to keep using a 24-inch bike, after I had grown out of it. And it was Michael's hand-me-down bike. I could barely show my face and drive it down the neighborhood streets. I knew everyone was laughing at me."

Michael: "That was a good bike, Richie. And when you complained, I offered to ride it and let you ride the one I bought with my own money from my paper route."

Esther: "Oh shut up Michael. Your false modesty is ugly."

Richie: "Yeah, shut up."

Gloria: "Ass kisser."

Eamon turned the page.

Bernie: "You are wrong, Gloria, the Rabbi was correct, not the school teacher, and you were wrong, too."

Audrey groaned and shook her head. She made a motion with her hands, signaling Eamon to turn back a page.

He turned back a page.

Bernie: "Oh, right . . . shut up, Michael."

Chapter 6

By intermission on the second night, the theater was only a quarter full. At the cast meeting afterwards, Audrey Sells quit the play with the words, "Nobody should have to put up with this. Come on everyone, let's go."

Eamon begged for calm. The lighting and sound tech, agreed to stay, and asked others to stay also. One by one, he got his cast back.

Eamon begged for somebody in the room to sit in tomorrow as Esther. He was met with silence. He begged. After he offered a dinner for two at the Hilton, a quiet, mousy retiree named Claudia, a volunteer costume maker, who had never acted in her life, agreed to play Esther. She worried that she wouldn't have time to learn any lines.

"Claudia, you have been here for every rehearsal. You know who Esther is deep down in your heart. Forget the lines and be her, be Esther, respond as Esther would respond. You will do great, Claudia. I have faith in you."

Eamon's suggestion changed the scope of the play. Nobody in the company cared for the play as it was. Allowing wholesale improvisation would be freeing. The actors playing the three Carp children were all college students, and they thought improv would be fun. The play couldn't get worse. Eamon smelled marijuana smoke on them. All agreed to help Claudia improv through the play.

The improvisation didn't work out well. During the next performance, number three, midway through the first act, Claudia took the insults against Esther personally. Her feelings were hurt. As the play continued. she became increasingly flustered. Finally she couldn't put together any lines.

Instead, she started bawling, loudly, sorrowfully, then she fled. As she ran off stage, Eamon, as Bernie, improvised, "Well, there she goes. Hope this time, she's gone for good."

Richie, heavily stoned: "You drove her off, you monster. How could you do that to my mother? Now I not only don't have a little brother, Saul, who is dead, but I don't have a mother. My own mother! You took my mother."

Chapter 7

On the fourth and final night of *Family Table*, with the grant money nearly in the bank, Eamon was sitting in the ticket booth, wearing a frumpy dress, selling no tickets, killing time before he would play Esther. The crew was thin. There was no sound and light tech. Eamon set the lights in one position for the performance. There would be no music, no sound effects.

The cast had agreed a half hour before the play that they would rather eliminate the loathsome Bernie character, than Esther, although the vote was rather close. Eamon, who was already dressed as Bernie, changed into a tight-fitting, thigh-length dress. He sat killing time in the ticket booth, the dress barely closed over his belly.

Only one person paid for tickets, a man who had been to all three previous shows, and who had praised the play after each performance in glowing online reviews. Later, after Eamon left the ticket booth to play Esther, a quartet of street kids entered with their backpacks and a pit bull, hoping for a dry spot out of the rain.

In the nearly empty theater, the thin, desperate and mostly stoned cast, spun out of control as the performers did battle on stage.

The improv explained that the father, Bernie, had been either assassinated by Chinese agents, had fallen into a vat of chemicals, had run off with his secretary, or had died from a horrible disease, depending on which character was speaking. Whatever the changing reason was that got rid of the old man, he was gone and all were glad.

The family was bickering less with Bernie gone. His departure had united them somewhat. Eamon, playing Esther, no longer used a falsetto.

When Richie asked about his baritone voice, Esther explained that his real name actually was Edward and that he was awaiting sex reassignment surgery.

When Gloria asked how he and Bernie could have had children, Eamon stammered for a moment then told them that all three kids were adopted. Edward and Bernie were young, in love, and it was the sixties. People did not come out of the closet back them.

Michael (stoned and giggling): "But I remember you pregnant with baby Richie."

Eamon shot him a look. *Give me a break.*

Esther: "I was wearing a pregnancy suit."

Gloria (laughing): What about that time when we went swimming at the YMCA. We changed in the locker room. I saw you naked!"

One of the street kids in audience exclaimed, "How do you explain that?"

Another street kid: "How do you hide your dick?"

From the top of the bleachers, a voice: "No no, she's a woman, Esther is a real woman. Bernie was a monster."

Esther, looking at the man said: "No, I'm not! I am a man. All man, always a man, regretfully a man, but soon, with surgery, I will be a woman."

Richie: "I don't believe you. You are my Mommy!"

Gloria: "I saw you taking a shower!"

Esther: "You are insane! I am a man!"

Richie: "You are a man? Who took a shower in the woman's locker room with my sister? Is that what you are saying . . . Daddy?"

Michael: "You are my Mommy! Please don't lie to me. I need a Mommy. Don't you love me?"

Richie: "Shut up, Michael."

Esther: "I am a man!"

Once again the man shouted from the audience: "You are not a man. You are a wonderful, misunderstood woman, and we all love you."

Michael: "Mommy? Daddy?"

Esther: "Man!"

Gloria: "Woman!"
Street Person: "Prove it! Pull down your pants!"

Chapter 8

Babe Hathaway's cable cooking show was taped in his Eugene home. The typical spring rain was making the trees move. The studio audience sat and waited. The show was about to begin.

The production assistant smiled and trained the small audience how to respond to the applause cards he held up. He spent a few minutes practicing with them.

"Very good, now Babe should be out in a few minutes, he'll say hello to you, his amazing studio audience, and introduce today's dish."

"What will he be doing today?"

"That's a secret. What fun would it be if I told you? I'll let Babe tell you. So hang tight and remember at the end of the show, you will each get to taste what he made. It should be delicious. I'll be back in just a minute. Thank you all for coming today. Let's make it a great show." He waved and left.

The film crew was making final lighting adjustments. The prep cook finished putting together the best-looking ingredients, while Babe sat in his downstairs office, fixing his hair, powdering his face, and putting on eyeliner and lip gloss.

He heard the audience shout: "COOKIN . . . WITH . . . BABE!" and started up the stairs.

"Babe Hathaway—Now That's Home Cookin," said the announcer.

"Babe" Hathaway smiled his biggest smile and exercised his rubbery face to warm up his facial muscles as he mounted the stairs.

Babe was blonde, 6'2" and looked like a surfer. He had acted and sung since childhood. At 35 years old, Babe had a great physical presence that had not helped his failed acting career.

When Babe stepped into the kitchen, up went the Big Round of Applause card and the tiny group sounded like a real TV audience.

"Thank you, thank you," the ever gracious host nodded and lifted his hands to quiet them.

"Thanks for coming today. It's a special time of year. The spring vegetables are starting to come to our tables at last. (Applause.)

"I know most of you are tired of eating the cabbage and kale and kohlrabi that have been available, now we are all very happy to see the return of young fresh leaves coming up in the garden. Like these microgreens, and some of the baby lettuce that has been planted by our great local farmers. Let's give them a hand. (Applause.) No more turnips and potatoes, not today. It's spring.

"Today we are going to make spring lasagna. And by the way, please remember that all the art work you see on these walls is made by local artists and each piece is for sale." The camera swept the paintings and small sculptures displayed in the living room. Each object had a small, white price sticker on it.

"These are beautiful works and they are all priced moderately. Just give me a call at the number shown and I will be happy to package up a lovely work of original art and ship it out to you. They are all looking for good homes. Thank you." Babe smiled and nodded into the camera.

"So let's talk lasagna. It is the quintessential Italian dish that has been interpreted over the years by millions of cooks worldwide. I would say it is a favorite of mine." He moved back into the kitchen. His apron was dark blue. It contrasted strongly with his bright blond hair. On it was embossed in wide silver letters, "COOKING WITH BABE".

Babe moved easily about the room picking up pans, and sliding cutting boards into view. The lights above were bright and his banter came and went in a rhythmic flow. One camera overhead showed Babe's hands working the ingredients and the pans. Two camera men roamed the area shooting Babe from a variety of angles. The editor sat at his console and chose the angle he wanted.

"The oven is preheated to 425°. All the ingredients are at room temperature. Take a long glass pan like this," he motioned to it, "and oil it with olive oil. How about a little background music? Maybe some light classical." The music came up on set. "That's good."

"I'm peeling the baby spring squash, slicing it very thin. I'm going to layer it with what some of you might consider an odd ingredient. You know those noodle sheets from the refrigerator section at the Asian store? Dip the whole mass into hot water for just a minute then set it on the board. Okay, then unroll it and put the noodle sheets between the layers of vegetables and sauce. Add a little grated cheese if you like.

As Babe moved around rapidly with grace and exuberance, his cell phone rang. He had forgotten to take it from his breast pocket. To get it from his pocket, he pushed the phone up from underneath. It slid through his fingers and plopped into the ever-present pot of boiling water. The ringing stopped.

"Oh well, I guess they can wait to talk to me until later." He chuckled, allowing the phone to continue boiling. The audience giggled.

"Well, moving on, the sauce is something I came up with a few years back when I was working on the set of a western movie. I played the part of the cook. Most of the time I had nothing to do but wait around the chuck wagon and pretend I was cooking, so I started to cook. This sauce is a version of what I thought might be possible with the ingredients the settlers brought with them."

Babe smiled and wiped his hands.

"The sauce I came up with is made from dried beef. I understand that the settlers made jerky, so I made a sauce using a variation of dried beef. You take the beef and put it into a small saucepan. Add to it a small amount of oil and heat it on low. The shredded beef will begin to absorb the oil and become soft as you work it for a few minutes. When it's soft, add just one clove of garlic finely chopped, and finish it with a squeeze of lemon. Now stir occasionally until it looks cloudy. Slowly add about two cups of water, and let it heat for about twenty minutes. Near the end, put in a quarter stick of butter. When it comes out of the oven, pour this over the top, spread it out well, and get it everywhere."

"The choice of cheese is important. Remember to play around, try out numerous cheeses."

Babe turned and grabbed the precooked lasagna out of the oven steaming and broadcasting a rich aroma throughout the room. (Applause.)

Close up on Babe's face.

"Thanks for coming to my kitchen today and sharing a meal with me. Goodbye, and always remember: put your heart into your cooking."

Theme music came up, with the applause, as Babe plated pieces of lasagna for his audience. The director signaled that the show is over. Everyone was sitting down, eating and talking.

Babe moved to the side of the kitchen and took off his microphone.

I love to cook, but I am so tired of having to do it as a hustle. So many gigs to juggle, just to eat and make the mortgage payment.

"Could I speak with you in private?"

Chapter 9

Babe turned around. A nicely dressed, middle-age woman touched him on the arm.

"My name is Ellen Madsen." She put out her hand. Babe shook it. He gestured for her to continue.

"I'm here for my sister, and for me. We have both suffered a terrible loss. We need your help, someone to investigate. The police stopped looking. Did you hear about Leo Laum, the young man who was run down on his bike a couple of weeks ago?"

"Yes of course. It was all over the news. Horrible, a hit and run, right?"

"That's what the police and the news are saying, but I don't believe it."

The woman solemnly shook her head.

"Joanna with the coastal artists' co-op told me I might call you. I can pay."

Babe remembered Joanna. She engaged him to investigate missing art. He took the case and discovered the thief was her son, angry about his curfew. He exposed the kid and she begged him to keep it quiet. Bottom line was she couldn't pay and offered him an amateurish piece of art as payment. It was now for sale on Babe's wall: a trophy wall of deadbeat artist clients.

Ellen Madsen looked like money.

He thought of his diminished wine cellar, his shockingly low bank balance, and the lack of acting, investigative jobs or even catering work recently. He needed to keep hustling despite how much it wore him down.

"I require a retainer, up front, and I work on an hourly or daily rate, your choice." He quoted a hefty advance and a high hourly rate. She didn't blink and reached for her checkbook.

"When can you begin?"

Babe imagined the comfort of a full bank account. He imagined foie gras, caviar, and a trip to Hawaii next winter.

As talented and well trained as Babe was, in both singing and acting, he had failed to make a living in the performing arts. If talent was the sole requisite for success, Babe would have been acting all the time. Instead, acting supplemented his primary jobs of cooking, catering, private investigations, even carpentry. Many years ago, the traveling musical that Babe was performing in went belly up in Vegas. Broke, alone and disillusioned, he hit bottom. Stranded in Vegas, Babe scoured the want ads and ended up working for a private investigator. He discovered he was good at it. After a while he got his own PI license and worked all kinds of cases, from insurance fraud to cheating spouses.

When his mom got sick and his professor dad passed, he left Vegas and spent three years caring for her in her large house on College Hill in Eugene, Oregon. He jumped into small town art and theater, and got his PI license in Oregon to pay his bills. After his mom died, he inherited her house and its mortgage payments. He networked his way into a TV show, "Cooking with Babe", to help pay for the house. However, he was always in a bind, hustling.

"I could talk to you now. Let's go downstairs to my office." He pointed the way.

"Excuse the mess." Babe cleared books off the second chair for her, and sat facing Ellen. "What's wrong with the police investigation? The Eugene police are usually good at what they do. On the news they seemed genuinely concerned."

"They talk the talk, but they seem to have given up. They don't believe me, they won't listen. That's what I need you for."

"To make them listen?"

"My nephew, Leo Laum, was not a nice person. Not at all."

"Yes?"

"He did bad things to a lot of people. He could be charming, talented, generous and wonderful. But he was cruel, and prone to thoughtless behavior. He had a trust fund from his grandfather, so he didn't need to work. He was active in the local theater. He was a dabbler, a volunteer. Unfortunately, he had a knack for insulting people, deeply. He's been like that since he was a kid. I think something was wrong with him. Some people even hated him. My own two children, his cousins, sorry to say, they hated him, and for good cause."

"And you think somebody might have disliked him enough to run him down?"

"I do." She leaned forward on her chair, hands on top of her legs. "That's exactly what I'm saying! It might have been deliberate. Yes! We just don't know. And Dory, my sister, needs closure, too. Can you help us?"

Babe pulled out the retainer form, filled it out and pointed out where to sign. They discussed the current state of the police investigation. Babe took notes.

"When can you get started?"

Babe smiled, thinking of earning decent money for a change.

"Well, what was he doing the night of his death, so late? He was hit in the wee hours, according to the paper."

"He was on the technical crew at the Eugene Experimental Theater. He did lights and sound work for their recent production of *Family Table*. He was going home. I guess you need to start there."

Babe groaned.

Ellen caught the groan.

"What?"

"Uh . . . nothing . . . I was thinking of . . . something else," Babe blurted, trying to cover his slip. He remembered reading the script for *Family Table*. He recalled deflecting the annoying sales pitch by the director, who called daily for two weeks, trying to woo him to play the part of the whining, abusive, disrespected, father, the loathsome Bernie. It was so bad the author published it under the name "Anonymous".

Oh no, why does it have to be Family Table.

It had taken every ounce of diplomacy to keep from telling the director the play was an awful piece of crap, so bad he would rather gouge out his own eyes with a plastic fork than be part of it.

Babe thought about his thin bank account.

"I'm ready to start today, as soon as they clear the house." He smiled his thousand-watt smile. For the first time, Ellen smiled a bit also. He stood up and held out his hand.

"Here's my card. So you have my phone number and email. Oh wait a minute. I just boiled my phone. Let me write down your number and I'll call you with my info as soon I get another one."

They shook hands and she turned to leave. He watched her leave.

Attractive in a mature hippy kind of way.

Chapter 10

"Eamon Krieg, please?"

Babe stood before the theater secretary, who wore gigantic glasses. Her wavy hair and freckled face bobbed like a sunflower in the waning days of summer. Unfortunately, her voice was not so lovely. It sounded like an aluminum flat-bottomed boat being pulled up a gravel launch ramp.

"Can I say who is calling?" She smiled.

"Babe Hathaway, uh, Donna." He responded, quickly reading the name plate on her desk.

She smiled, flattered by the superficial intimacy of having her name spoken. Instead of pressing the button on an intercom and announcing Babe's arrival, Donna swiveled in her chair and called out.

"Eamon!" Babe imagined a painful fog of pulverized rock dust coming from her throat as she called out.

"Donna. I'm right here; you really don't have to shout so loud. Could you give me a break?" Eamon appeared in the doorway to the right of Donna's desk, a file folder in hand. He had met Eamon before, months ago, when they had talked about the possibility of Babe being part of *Family Table*, by Anonymous.

"Eamon, I'd like to have a word with you about Leo Laum. Do you have the time to talk?"

"I have all the time in the world. We can speak out on the deck if you like."

Babe followed Eamon out the double doors to a patio on the side of the building, and they sat at one of the intermission refreshment tables. Eamon was tall and thin except for a protruding belly. He had a shock of red, kinky hair that festooned like a bouquet from the top of his head. His features were small and refined, and his long thin hands and mannerisms reminded Babe of an Anglican preacher he once saw at a funeral many years ago.

"What can I do for you, Babe?"

"I need to talk to you about Leo Laum."

"Oh yes, Leo. Dreadful event, his untimely passing, wasn't it?" He looked down and shook his head.

"Ellen Madsen hired me to look into it. She thinks the cops are done with it, put it aside. She thinks it was a murder."

"A murder? You really think so?"

"Possibly so, he may have been targeted, singled out, stalked."

"Who could have done such an awful thing?"

Babe heard hollowness in the reply. It didn't ring true.

"That's why I'm here. You know the crew and the cast. You know who Leo knew and maybe you know someone who had a motive. Anyone you know angry with him?"

Eamon looked away. He waited a minute before answering, biting his lower lip.

"Oh shit, Babe, at one time or another, everyone was pissed off at that scoundrel. Even me, I have to admit. But . . . I didn't kill him." He looked off over the hedges that separated the theater from the auto repair place next door.

"What do you mean everyone was pissed off at him?"

"Leo was a joker. He carried the day, if you know what I mean. He had to have his hand in the mix, no matter what was going on. He put permanent inks in the makeup jars and we had to perform a show in blue face one night. It could have all gone downhill until we figured out a way to sell it as an avant garde approach to the classic play. The actors were nuts. They had to cover the blue with flesh tones in order to keep their day jobs. They all looked like zombies during the day." He smiled and chuckled.

"It turned out to be a brilliant coup. We were written up in the journal from Ashland Oregon's Shakespeare Theater. They thought it was a new take on an old piece. Maybe Leo was a genius. Mostly everyone thought he was hostile, treacherous and annoying."

"What about enemies?"

He shook his head. "Take your pick, Babe. Anyone could have done it, but his actions weren't really overly harsh as far as I know. You will need to talk to some folks."

"Good, maybe you can bring me a list? I'm reaching out to you for some guidance on this." At this moment, Babe could see Eamon interlacing his fingers and leaning forward to speak. He imagined the priestly collar, the understanding eyes, even an Irish lilt in his voice. But none of that was forthcoming.

"What am I, the cops?" Eamon barked with way too much energy and hostility. He got up and faced the wall. "Get your own fucking list. I've got work to do."

Eamon paused and relented.

"Okay, sorry for the outburst. Donna will give you a list of everyone who works here. You can nose around all you want."

Babe saw that Eamon was losing his temper for some reason. He decided to push further and see what he might get.

"Well Jesus, Eamon, isn't there anyone you know who Leo rubbed the wrong way?"

"Let me think about this for a day. We'll get you a list."

"Anything you can help me with would be greatly appreciated."

"There were some issues with the lighting guy, I seem to remember. Let me see what I can do."

Babe left. He was glad to get out of there.

Chapter 11

Twenty minutes later, Babe sat at Tommy's Place, a small drinking establishment named after a beloved local alcoholic, Tommy. Everybody loved Tommy, except of course, his wife and kids. Behind the bar there were photos of Tommy shaking hands with almost everyone.

There was a sepia photo framed with Tommy and General Eisenhower, a shot in Vegas with Frank Sinatra, a portrait of Tommy with his two kids and his wife sitting in front of the statue of Lincoln, and a much older Tommy with a perplexed expression being introduced to James Brown.

It was clear that Tommy had been everywhere, including jail. Tommy had been "connected". But that was a long time ago. The Cosa Nostra was over. Organized crime was no longer about killing people, it was about dumping garbage at sea, avoiding cigarette taxes, and getting paid off for looking the other way.

Babe liked Tommy's Place. It was friendly and they had a great variety of scotch. Best of all, it was within walking distance from his house. That's what really counted. He could drink as much as he liked and walk home. In case he couldn't walk home, there was a lovely grassy field beside the bar where he could find a soft spot and fall asleep.

"Can I borrow your phone?" He asked the bartender.

"You mean my cell phone or the house phone?"

"Do you have a house phone?"

"We do have one. We don't have a pay phone anymore. We took that out years ago. No one used it. You need the house phone?"

He pointed to a wait station that held bottles of ketchup, large pepper grinders, napkins, and so on. Beside the station was a wall phone. In the quiet alcove, Babe walked the long cord as far as it could go to the back wall and dialed Lars, his I.T. guy. Lars was far more than an Internet tech. He was a hacker who could work around innumerable fire walls on local, federal and international levels. He was a diamond in the rough, sometimes very rough.

"Lars, it's Babe, I need your help?"

"Are you in jail again? I can't do that kind of funds transfer anymore. They blocked that pathway. But if it's cash you need, let me know, I can work something out."

"Lars, I'm not in jail. I need a cell phone. I boiled mine."

"How did it taste?"

"I don't have the time to get a new one. I need it for business. You said something about used phones last time we talked. Can you get me one?"

"I've got a few here. Come on by and I'll hook you up. They're pretty new. I got one that was repo'd. They didn't pay the bill, and the company took it back. They don't want to use it again, so guess who bought it for a discount, a deep discount? Come by, I'll clean it up for you."

"Okay, save it for me, it may take me a few days to get up there."

Babe hung up the phone and looked around with suspicion. After talking to Lars, he felt he was in a B movie being tailed.

Chapter 12

The new Eugene Police Station was located across the road from a country club. Babe Hathaway parked his restored 1967 Dodge Dart convertible in the parking lot. He stood in the cool drizzle and admired his vintage car for the hundredth time. It was one of the last American cars with a hood ornament. It had a reliable slant six engine, and a dashboard-mounted, pushbutton automatic transmission. Babe was the second owner. In spite of its age, it had only 85,000 miles on the original engine.

He stepped around puddles, entered the lobby, and informed the receptionist he was here for his meeting. She buzzed him through to an office, and Lieutenant Carl Carenza, the lead investigator on Leo Laum's case, waved him to a seat. He didn't get up. Carenza was heavyset, late forties, a man aging badly: short graying hair and swollen veins on the surface of his nose. Pictured behind him was a young Carenza in full uniform shaking hands with a police chief. No family photos.

He looked up from his paperwork at Babe with dull, suspicious hound dog eyes, as if Babe had a trunk full of kidnapped children outside.

Babe took him in at a glance and went into improv mode. He tightened his facial features into a pained scowl that matched Carenza's, and lumbered, like a much heavier man might, to the chair. He sat with a slight grunt and matched Carenza's body posture. He held out a card. Carenza sat back and made no move to take it. Babe put the card on the desk.

"Who hired you?" said Carenza.

"Ellen Madsen."

"Who's she?"

Babe was momentarily stunned.

"Leo's aunt, his mother's sister."

Carenza let out a derisive snort. He stared at Babe.

Babe stared back.

"What's that mean?" asked Babe.

Carenza kept his stone-faced stare. Finally, tiring of this, Carenza snorted again.

"Did anyone interview her?" said Babe.

"No."

Babe felt anger, and put it into his stare, understanding what the Laum family was going through.

"Are you going to?"

Carenza shrugged.

"Yeah. Okay. Give me the number." He tossed a legal pad onto a stack of files in front of Babe. Babe wrote the number and tossed the pad back.

Babe decided he would push Carenza's buttons. He leaned forward, hands on his knees.

"She said the police don't care. You've concluded that it was just a hit and run. You've stopped looking. Why's that?"

"That what she said? That we don't care? That we stopped looking?" Color rose into Carenza's face.

"That's right. Why don't you tell me what you do know? Give me a place to start."

Carenza now leaned forward. He looked ready to hurl his heavyweight body across the desk at Babe.

"Figures."

"What's that mean? You said you didn't talk to her," said Babe.

"Let me tell you something." Carenza jabbed a finger at Babe.

He seemed to be searching for words. Finally he put his hand on the desk.

"We care."

"Okay."

"Do you understand that? We care. We haven't stopped looking, even though I have two other high-profile cases. I don't appreciate hearing this accusation one single bit. This is not a good thing."

What's Carenza's problem?

Babe sat back, lightened up, and adopted a friendly, open posture.

"I can help. Maybe a fresh pair of eyes will help."

"Knock yourself out. Just don't ruin my case."

"What case?"

Carenza flushed deeper red.

Babe decided to try another direction.

"Ellen said she obtained permission for me to look at the file. Where should I start looking?"

"I didn't get a release. So I can't show you the file. It's an ongoing investigation."

"Until then, just give me a place to start."

Carenza sat back. He looked up for a long moment. Babe thought the sound of violins at this juncture might help his cause.

"Aren't you going to give me any help? They lost their son! Can you imagine the horror they are going through?" Babe warbled lyrically.

Carenza looked at Babe with a sinister smile.

"Go talk to Leo Laum's family. Talk to them. Go ahead."

"What about the theater employees? Ms. Madsen said Leo had enemies. What did you find out from the people in the play? They knew that Leo would be riding his bike home late at night"

Carenza shook his head.

"Nothing there, we met them. Some people didn't care for him, but there didn't seem to be any real threats."

Carenza looked down at the file open in front of him, signaling the end of the interview.

"Will you keep me up to date, if anything new comes up?" asked Babe.

Carenza inhaled deeply, and let it out in a slow hiss.

"What's your problem, Lieutenant? I'm just trying to help a grieving family deal with an unimaginable personal loss, at no cost to the city, and I can't get the time of day from you. What's your problem?"

"I got no problem, but maybe I'm going to have a problem—with you. I got work to do now. We care. But let me tell you something: Make sure you let me know if you find something out. Go talk to the family."

He smiled his grimace and chinned Babe toward the door.

Chapter 13

Babe called the Laum home from his land line. It reminded him that he had a new/used iPhone waiting for him at Lars' place.

"Laum residence, Susie speaking." She picked up after the first ring, as if she had been sitting by the phone. There was desperation in her voice.

"This is Babe Hathaway. I'm a P.I. and I'm looking into the death of your brother. I would like to come by to ask your family a few questions."

"Well we spoke to the cops already but sure, come by. We watch you on TV. I think your cooking shows are fun. I never tried to make any of it, but it looks like it tastes good."

"You are welcome to come down to the studio and sit in on a session, you know. It is indeed a lot of fun."

Maybe you'll buy some of the awful artwork on the walls.

"I guess I could do that. Maybe I could get on camera for a moment when you show the studio audience. That would be worth going for. I want to be famous, but not for cooking. I'm really quite attractive and I can sing, too. I'm in the chorus now and working my way up to doing a solo act."

"I see. That sounds wonderful." Babe was reminded by her overly eager voice of so many young actresses he had known. He had been around countless theater groups and events that attracted this type of personality. She was the actress determined to convince the world she was terrific, not by great performances but by her own agitated self-description.

"Is it possible that I might stop by? Is it alright with your family? Will they be home within the next little bit?" Babe queried.

"We don't ever go anywhere, and I have so much practice to catch up on. Do you have any leftovers from the show? My folks will be really hungry as soon as they see you. They watch the cooking shows and the next thing you know they're in the kitchen making a snack. But they're terrible cooks. They think they're great but the food is awful. I have to bring in take-out just to keep my guts from running."

Too much information.

"Well, maybe I can cook something while I'm there."

"Oh would you? That would be great. I'll tell mom and dad. They'd love it."

Babe could hear her yelling with a hand over the phone, asking if Babe can come over to cook for them and ask stuff about Leo. Babe shook his head thinking he was in over his head. After years of being pounded by the ruthless ambitions of others in the theatrical community, Babe had learned the correct posture required to be heard and to prevail. Susie's voice had reminded him to be vigilant.

Chapter 14

Babe rang the bell. He carried with him a small pad and a bag with onions, cooked rice, eggs, some broccoli and his own wok. He was taking the show on the road. Susie opened the door instantly. She stood in front of him like a Valkyrie or a ship's prow ornament. She looked at him as if from high above. She projected grandeur.

"Won't you come in, Babe? I'm Susie, ever so pleased to actually meet you."

Babe nodded. Thinking her speech was conceived to sound like an invitation to an English garden party at which older folks spoke insincerely and with great respect for style—the kind of party at which nothing was said. It was all about the tea and the loveliness of the afternoon and Aunt Henny's new smock.

"Thank you for allowing me to come by to talk with you." He extended his hand to shake.

From behind Susie, Mrs. Laum crowded in over her shoulder. Her grey head bobbed as she peered steadily at Babe.

"You look just like you do on TV," she said.

"Mrs. Laum, how nice of you to ask me over, and I've brought some cooking materials in case we get a bit peckish." Babe continued with the English tea party style.

"Call me Dory, everyone calls me Dory. It's really Doris, but that's what they call me." Her eyes fluttered. For a moment Babe thought she might have been flirting with him. Perhaps it was just her style.

They went into the open living room and Mr. Peter Laum stood from his seat on the couch. He was a large pear shaped man. His distended belly was carried about like a cultural artifact that exhibited how financial success and gluttony were one and the same. His form was thick and full in honor of his ability to afford the good things in life. He was proud of his breadth. He looked at Babe suspiciously.

"Pleased to meet you, Mr. Babe." He reached out his large, flaccid hand for a handshake. His eyes bored into Babe's, full of mistrust.

"Well I've brought some stuff to cook for us. I hope that after we talk we can sit down for a light meal."

"Let me take that stuff from you." Dory grabbed the bag from Babe and retreated to the kitchen. Babe saw her slight resemblance to Ellen Madsen.

"Have a seat." Peter motioned toward the couch. Babe scoped the positioning of the chairs. He realized that if he sat on the couch he would be dominated by Mr. Laum and would not be heard. He took a small side step and sat on the chair across from the couch. It put him in the right spot to lead the proceedings. Peter showed a slight cheek wiggle in reaction to Babe's disobedience.

"Susie, Dory? Get in here, so this guy can interview us. Let's get it going if we want to have some of his food." He shouted this though the Laum women were only steps away in the kitchen. He had become a town crier.

When Babe sat down, Leo's father talked about his life. He had spent many years building his own father's furniture business. He had always loved furniture. He talked about bedding and the value of a good night's sleep. Babe had to stop him.

"And you Dory? Did you work in the furniture business with your husband?" Mr. Laum looked upset that his speech was interrupted. Babe had to do something to stop him or he would never ask questions about Leo.

"No I never worked there. I was too busy taking care of the children. There's Javier the oldest. He left the nest early. I called him that because I had romantic feelings for Ricardo Montalban. Mmm mmm." She slapped her backside, and glanced across the table at Peter throwing a sultry lift of her eyebrow at him.

"We call him Javra. That was little Leo's first way of saying his big brother's name. Javra's down in Florida, Cape Coral. He's a successful chiropractor. Always kept to himself, never married. Had a girlfriend for a while but it ended after a couple of years. I hear from Javra about once a year. I wish he called more often,

but he doesn't. What are you gonna do? He's quiet. Not like Leo .
. ."

"They hated each other," interrupted Peter.

Babe was startled by his rudeness. "Who?"

"Leo and Javra. Couldn't stand each other. Fought all
the time."

"Oh my baby! My poor baby," moaned Dory.

"Oh shut up, Dory," barked Peter.

Dory's tearfulness disappeared in an instant, turning to fury.
"Who are you to tell me not to be sad, you pathetic little man?"

Susie grinned and looked at Babe.

Babe decided to try to steer the conversation back.

Maybe she really is devastated.

"Tell me about Leo. Did he have a lot of friends?"

"Everybody liked Leo because he partied." Susie interjected.
"But he was a putz."

"No enemies at all, and he liked having a good time," said
Dory.

"He had his problems. Not overeating, like mom and dad,
but he was angry. He was in therapy early, maybe since he was a
teenager. Isn't that right mom?" said Susie.

Dory was still glaring at her husband, seeing if he wanted to
go another round. She turned to Babe.

"Well, he did go to the school counsellor at first, but it didn't
seem to help at all."

"Oh, come on. Just say it! He was a nasty, mean spirited
putz." Peter Laum chimed in, "He played a lot of practical jokes,
especially on Javra."

"He was jealous. It was obvious," said Susie. "Javra was
handsome and Leo was a slob."

"Oh my poor little slob Leo."

Peter shot her a look, and she glared back at him.

"What kind of practical jokes?" asked Babe.

Mrs. Laum smiled brightly. She jumped on it.

"I remember when he was little. He knew that Javra loved to
put a lot of sugar in his tea. Leo took a bowl and put it on the
table with salt in it. Javra just grabbed the bowl and put in a good
couple of spoonfuls into his tea. He spit it all out. We found out

after the fact. We were sitting in the dining room and they were in the kitchen. Apparently Leo stuck around to watch it happen, he was taking his time putting together his breakfast just to see Javra suffer."

"He was an annoying little shit sometimes," Peter said, his eyes teary with fondness.

"You said he went to a doctor. Can you give me the name of the doctor? Maybe he can shed light on some aspect of Leo's personality that could help me find his . . . I mean find out who did this to your son."

"You mean his killer. He was killed wasn't he? It wasn't an accident like the police said?" said Susie.

"That's what I'm looking into. I don't know. It might be someone he knew. I want to get a list of his friends." Babe poised to write down names.

"There wasn't anybody close. He knew everybody but no one ever came by to visit him here, maybe they did at his apartment. He was too much of a jerk to have real friends. People took advantage of his generosity." Susie obviously missed him. It was a mixed bag: Leo was fun and he was a pain in the ass.

"Leo didn't live here with us. I was at his apartment a couple of times. He threw a party here for the theater crew and cast. I thought it might be a good place to meet guys. It was crowded. I got felt, you know hands up the skirt in the hallway. It was fun, got me randy. You should talk to his roommates. But Leo was deep; he had his tongue in his cheek most of the time. No one noticed. He loved the theater, ever since he was a kid." Susie said.

Dory nodded her head and teared up as she spoke.

"Oh for the love of God, dry it up, Dory," said Peter.

Dory ignored him this time. "I remember how he would put on plays in the backyard. He started when he was about six. One time he played his dad. Remember that, Peter? How he put on that big jacket and had his friends move a table around as if he was you at the shop having the guys move a table into a room so the clients could have a better look at it."

Peter nodded. His hands were across his chest sternly preventing the outpouring of his heart.

Babe got the name of his current roommates and the name of the doctor.

"Why did he go to the doctor?"

"He was angry all the time." Dory said.

"He started at about twelve getting really angry and snippy and aggressive with everyone. He hit some kid at school. They had been arguing on the playground and Leo hauled off and socked him one. They called me at the store and I had to go in."

"I remember it clear as day: I could have sold a dining room set that day; the little shit caused me to miss the sale, two thousand bucks down the drain. They never came back," said Peter bitterly.

"Leo's anger? I never got to the bottom of it, and it became more frequent. The school psychologist suggested a meeting with a private counsellor and Leo went for about a year off and on. He hated it at first, and then he seemed to really like it, but that failed and we got him this new age Doctor. He really liked him."

"Yeah right," said Susie raising her voice. "He used his sessions as a time to be dramatic. He'd tell the doctor stories and it made him feel important. He told me once that he pulled the wool over the doctor's eyes. He was bragging about it."

Babe suggested he begin to cook.

"Get the table set, Dory, supposedly we got a real cook in the house. Don't ever eat her cooking, you'll regret it." Peter said.

"Let's put out the good china. This is an occasion." Dory shuffled around the dining room.

"What are you making?" demanded Peter.

"I thought we could have a light meal, broccoli and onions, with stir fried rice and eggs."

"What? Eggs? That's breakfast. I want chicken. You hear that, Dory?"

Babe could hear them ordering each other around and complaining. It was difficult to be around. Susie stood too close to him as he prepared to cook. He put on his apron and assembled the food on the counter beside the stove.

"Leo had some weird habits," Susie said, while idly handling the knives Babe had set out.

"He used to shave all the time. The family's kind of hairy, ya know? I mean, I'm a big girl and it's all muscle." Susie pulled up her sleeve and made a muscle. Babe looked over and saw her bulging bicep.

"You must work out hard."

"I dance, that's all. It keeps me in shape. I don't look hairy but I am in one spot. Look." Susie pulled up her shirt and showed Babe a small trail of soft brown hair that ran downward from her belly button.

"It goes all the way down." She began to pull down her sweat pants.

"I get it. You don't have to show me." Babe turned toward the cutting board.

What is it with this family?

He took a step away from Susie and began to cut the broccoli and onions.

"You're not like the other food show host on cable. We sometimes watch her, the heavy-set English lady. She makes some tasty stuff. It makes me sad though to watch her over the years." Susie moved around while she spoke.

Babe found it unnerving. It was as if she was about to lick his face.

"She keeps cooking really rich and fatty food. And she cooks for all the neighbors in her fancy neighborhood. Then her husband comes home and she dotes on him. They seem to love each other and it's kind of sweet, but she just keeps getting fatter and her voice is so cloying. It's sad. You know she's going to die from eating all that rich heavy food and she has gotten so fat over the years. It's like watching a slow motion car accident. I had to stop watching it. My folks still watch it. I just leave the room."

Slow motion car accident. How did Leo get hit? What really happened?

"Have you considered moving out? Getting your own place?"

"Sure I have. But they wouldn't be able to get by here without me. With Leo gone, I bring them joy. I'm like their morning light."

'Their morning light'? She's like living theater. But maybe that's a key to who Leo was.

Babe finished a quick wok meal in minutes. Dory and Peter were arguing about where each person should sit. Peter insisted that Babe sit at the head of the table as the guest of honor. Dory preferred a simpler pattern of two across from two, with Susie next to Babe because he was an eligible and attractive man who might fancy Susie. She even suggested that this could be the man who would marry their Susie.

"Who wants her? She's too pushy."

"Shush Peter. Don't say that. Maybe Babe will find her appealing. After all she is really well built and knows her way around the bedroom." She rolled her eyes seductively at her husband who grimaced.

"Stop that Dory. You're getting me excited. We have a guest. Settle down."

"Shut up Peter. You know you like it." He grabbed her hair and forced her head back, dominating her. He let go when he saw Babe and Susie walk into the dining room with the food.

"Here we are, broccoli, egg and onion-fried rice," said Babe, setting the platter on the table."

Peter looked at the food suspiciously. "Broccoli? I hate broccoli. Why couldn't you make chicken? What's wrong with a nice roast chicken?"

Susie scooped a large helping and passed the platter to Peter, who was mumbling to himself. He took a tiny amount and passed it to Dory, who took a small spoonful.

Susie took a bite and stared at Babe while she licked her lips. "Delightful. Mmmmm."

Peter took a tiny taste, and pushed his plate away.

"Achhh, I can't eat this. This isn't food. Dory, do we have any soup left?" He sat back with his hands folded over his big belly.

Dory sprang to her feet and ran into the kitchen. Babe heard the sound of an electric can opener. Susie slowly took another bite, licked her lips and shot bedroom eyes at Babe.

Chapter 15

Babe picked up his new/used phone, meeting Lars in a strange location that Lars insisted on, a parking lot behind a thrift store in West Eugene. Knowing that Lars sometimes exhibited paranoid tendencies, Babe agreed to go there without comment. Then it took him an hour while sitting at a coffee shop to grasp the basics. He figured out how to use the mapping function and set the address for Leo's last residence. He had not had time to give out the phone number to anyone.

Time to pay a visit.

The voice on the GPS told him that he had arrived at his destination. He pulled to the side of the quiet residential street and turned the car off. "Hawkins Place Quads, Luxury Student Living *at an* affordable price." He looked up and felt the sun on his face, maple and oak trees towering above him. The afternoon air smelled fresh after a recent rain.

He thought about the case and his meeting with the Laum family. He shuddered and made a grunting, vomiting sound, as if he could expel his ugly memory of that toxic family. He was shocked that there was such theatricality about the Laums' sadness. They seemed to be faking it. It was a house of self-absorbed, miserable, fucks.

Fuck them, fuck Leo, fuck 'em all.

He shook his head. He didn't really care who killed Leo. He was curious about it now, but it didn't matter. The idea of quitting and driving away was far more appealing. He could be at the coast in about an hour or so.

Maybe I'll call Terri, see if she can meet me at a restaurant for oysters and champagne.

Babe quickly remembered his thin finances. He would have to give back the advance check. He looked at his notebook: this is it. The roommates were expecting him.

Quad D was in front of him. Cedar walls, tile roof, multi-storied, extending down a hillside, a two-car garage at street level on top. It was a modern-style building in the midst of a lovely old neighborhood, an incongruent eyesore. He remembered his own noisy boy-squalor college days in dorms and apartments. This is luxury.

A tall young man in tennis whites, with an upper-class bearing and a sweater thrown over his shoulder, opened the door.

Oh Biff, is Muffy home? Be a dear and fetch her.

"I'm Babe Hathaway, we spoke?" he said, extending his hand.

"Uh no, you spoke to Robert, my roommate. I'm Taylor Colgate, pleased to meet you."

He led the way down a flight of stairs to a living room with a picture window overlooking west Eugene and the tops of tall firs almost close enough to reach.

A thin, dark haired young man arose slowly and gracefully from the couch.

"Robert Evans."

Babe shook his moist hand. Babe sized him up.

"You a dancer?" asked Babe.

"Why yes, good eye. I dance with a club at the university a little bit, for fun, but my MFA will be in studio production and computer graphics. I figured that's where the money is when I graduate."

Babe nodded. "Better odds."

Robert shrugged. "I love your show."

"Thanks, I appreciate you taking the time to talk to me." Babe sat at the dining room table and took out a yellow legal pad.

"As I mentioned over the phone, the Laum Family hired me to look into Leo's death."

Taylor and Robert looked at each with puzzled expressions.

"Who hired you?"

"Why, Leo's aunt Ellen hired me."

"Oh, okay," said Taylor, as if this solved a big mystery.

"What was that look you just exchanged?"

Taylor waited a moment, gathered his thoughts.

"I can't imagine the Laums hiring anyone. Their priorities are a little, shall we say, unusual."

Babe changed the subject.

"This is a lovely place, fabulous view. Is this a quad?"

"Yes, but just the two of us live here now, since Leo's accident, and Tim leaving," said Taylor. Robert nodded.

"You think it was an accident?" said Babe.

"Well sure. That's what the police said in the papers. We talked to them," said Robert, looking suddenly upset.

"Well, I've been hired to go a little deeper if I can. The police aren't helping me. The officer I talked to got upset when I mentioned the Laums. He sent me to talk to them. They weren't much help."

Taylor and Robert looked at each other again, and snickered.

"You know Leo's parents?"

They nodded.

"And Susie?"

Robert grimaced and Taylor started shaking his head, singing in a child's voice: "Robert and Susie, sitting in a tree, k-i-s-s-i-n-g . . . "

"Come on. Knock it off!" Robert complained sharply.

"Sorry," said Taylor shaking his head. "Sorry Robert, I must be channeling my inner Leo."

They looked at each other.

"Fuckin' Leo," they said in unison.

Babe looked at his notes. "Let's start with where each of you were on the night Leo died, somewhere between 2 and 3 a.m.?"

"We were here, both of us, all night long," said Robert, and Taylor nodded.

"I think we both went to bed around 11 p.m. I remember the news was just coming on," said Taylor.

"That's right," said Robert.

"We had a couple of beers earlier, watched some TV, went to our rooms," said Taylor.

"It wasn't my night to work the lights at the theater," said Robert. "It was Leo's night. Leo did the lighting and sometimes the sound on Friday and Saturday, and I had Sunday matinee and Sunday night. So I was off that night."

Babe looked at his other questions.

"I was hired to look at this as a possible homicide, regardless of what the cops think."

"You think he was killed?" said Robert. His lower lip began quivering. For a second it looked like he might start to cry. Then it passed.

"I don't know. I'm trying to find out. You knew him. Did he have any enemies? What was he like?"

Taylor looked up at the ceiling. "He was complicated." He stood, walked over to a door that opened from the narrow hall beside the living room.

"Leo could be a real nice guy, a generous, fun person, great company. But if he decided he didn't like you, you might as well leave, don't even pack. Look at this."

Babe watched Taylor open the door. Babe could see into the room. It was full of boxes, furniture, and a bicycle.

"This is Tim's room. He went home to Connecticut after what Leo did to him. He pretty much left everything here."

"Did the police question Tim?"

"I don't know. He changed his phone number, his email addresses. He won't talk to us."

"Do you think Tim could be involved with Leo's death?"

"Who knows? I'm sure Tim wouldn't be broken up about it. Probably relieved," said Taylor.

"What happened between them?"

Taylor shook his head sadly. "If Tim had just moved out when Leo asked, it could have been avoided."

Robert nodded.

"The four of us: Leo, Tim Hindler, Robert and I met on the university student housing website. We thought it would work out, so we took this place on a year lease. We moved in and discovered that Tim Hindler had big time ambitions to be in an orchestra, and he had to play the violin for hours a day. He was practicing all the time. He won awards in high school. He was really talented. Leo's room was right below Tim's and the violin drove him crazy. Leo couldn't get away from it. The walls are thin. This place looks new and nice but it's very cheaply made. Leo asked us to trade rooms with him. Robert's room and my room block out the sound pretty much, since we are on the other side of the house. We said no. Then Leo asked Tim to move out, but Tim said no. His room has the same lovely view as this living room, and he said it inspired his music. He got stubborn about it. Leo went to the landlord, and asked if Leo could break the lease and leave. The landlord said no, said he was responsible for the full year, even if he left, and if he left, he would be sued. Most landlords who deal with student housing have to be tough but this was ridiculous."

"The landlord got four slashed tires a month later," said Robert. "Leo could be vicious."

"What he did to the landlord was nothing compared to what he did to Tim."

"What did he do?"

Taylor snorted. "What didn't he do? It went on and on. You have to understand, Leo had a gift for finding weakness and exploiting it."

Babe nodded.

With parents like his, I'm surprised Leo wasn't a murderer.

"Let's see. First, Leo short-sheeted Tim's bed."

"He put butter in Tim's hairbrush. He made fun of Tim's lisp," said Robert.

"It wasn't that bad of a lisp."

"Leo kept mocking him with the phrase, 'Hindler's Lisp'," said Robert.

"Tim was vain about his looks, but he was shy and had trouble meeting girls. Leo hooked Tim up with an unattractive blind date," said Taylor.

"Leo convinced Tim to sign up for a dating site. He helped Tim set up the account. Meanwhile, Leo opened his own account pretending to be a woman and contacted Tim. He seduced Tim and persuaded him to take lewd pictures of himself. I remember Leo showing me his request: 'Let me see your ass.'"

"Leo posted Tim's pictures online. The entire campus saw them. That was rough," said Robert.

Taylor pointed his finger up, remembering more. "He sent a phony sweepstakes-winning letter to Tim. Got him believing he won a quarter million dollars. Tim was so sensitive and gentle. By the time he realized Leo was after him, he didn't know what to do to make it stop. He tried to move out, but the landlord refused. He stopped playing his violin and apologized, but Leo wouldn't stop."

"Leo was on a roll." Robert had his head down, and was shaking it back and forth.

"When Leo figured out Tim wouldn't fight back, he started calling him 'Timid' instead of Tim."

"Tim was miserable. He wasn't sleeping, or eating. Tim drove back home, all the way to Connecticut. He never came back. His stuff is still here. Leo then filed a lawsuit for the monthly rent. Tim never showed up in court, so Leo sent a collection agency looking for him."

"I've heard enough. Why did you put up with him?"

They looked at each other, as if the question never occurred to them.

"He wasn't bothering us, only Tim. He was cool to us. We had fun, some laughs, and wild parties. One especially great party for the theater cast and crew was at his parent's house. I'll never forget that one."

Taylor looked at Robert. "What a party. Nobody is going to forget that night."

Robert shook his head.

"Leo made this punch that must have had a ton of 190 proof alcohol in it. There was nothing else to drink at the party. You couldn't taste the alcohol; it was so full of fruit flavor. About 25 people got blasted, including his parents. Then his parents had this huge screaming argument in the kitchen. Leo made it a point to get everyone to watch them. Nobody missed a word as they viciously attacked each other. His parents suddenly stopped ranting and started kissing and groping each other in plain view."

"Oh no," said Robert.

"While the parents were going at it, Leo's sister Susie grabbed Robert and they started making out. You loved it, right?"

"It was kind of hot, at the time."

"Leo tormented Robert about that too. Susie and Robert, sitting . . . ."

"Stop it!"

"Sorry."

"How about the theater? Did he get along with people there?"

"I heard a story that he scared some guy real bad. Some Leo prank. Luckily the guy didn't get hurt."

Another suspect.

"Anybody else who might have been angry with him?"

"I can't think of anybody. I guess it sounds pretty bad. Maybe we should have stopped him, especially about Tim."

"You think?" asked Babe

Assholes!

"I was hoping Taylor would say something," said Robert.

"Now that he's gone, after seeing what he did to Tim, I guess we were both a little afraid of Leo."

"Is there anybody else who might be able to tell me about Leo and his life? He must have had enemies."

"Do you think he was murdered?" Robert asked.

"I don't know. I already dislike him," said Babe. "After talking to you, I'm not ruling anything out."

"Talk to Leo's counselor, Dr. Ernie, he must have known Leo pretty well. Leo went to counselling once a week. He told me he had been going for years, different counselors, they didn't seem to stay around, kept dropping Leo as a client, he would go out and find another, and the parents would insist on paying for it. Dr. Stinky, that's what Leo called Dr. Ernie," snickered Taylor.

"Or Dr. Pony sniffer," said Robert. They burst out laughing at that one.

Something odd is really going on, thought Babe, "Why did Leo go to these counselors?"

"Leo said his parents paid for the whole thing. They wanted to cure Leo of his sadness. They had been told that it was the cause of his anger somehow, that's how Leo explained it. They wanted to save him, as if that were possible. They would do anything. He played them like a fiddle. He made them believe his problems were their entire fault. They ate it up. He manipulated them into spending thousands. It made him feel powerful, in control. He was a savage genius I tell you. Leo made sure they wasted their money for his amusement. He was in the driver's seat."

Taylor laughed at Leo's devious anger. Robert snickered quietly with amusement.

"What a crackup!" blurted Taylor " . . . Geez . . . the shit he said and did. He had us rolling on the floor sometimes, it was so funny. What an absurd sense of humor, a tormented comic. I swear to God. If he could have gotten past his odd aggressive streak, he could have been the next great comic. He was that good. And believe it: his family is really fucked up, and at this point, who knows how much of that was Leo's doing. What it must have been like for those two monster parents of his to be in control of little baby Leo. They didn't know what they were creating."

Taylor chuckled to himself, thinking of something else.

"I just remembered: Leo was banned from every comedy club in Eugene, Salem and Portland. He never performed on stage at any of them, but he was banned because he was a heckler. It started almost innocently: One comic, I think his name was Buddy Shekfield or something, paid him to heckle his competition, drive them away. Leo did it. His heckling stole the show that night, and he heckled every comic, but the one guy, whose act Leo loved, he howled with laughter and supported his jokes, the audience loved it. I videotaped it. We flooded YouTube with short clips of Leo and the comics and the audience. Good footage. He took the club over and became a mini sensation on the Internet at least for a few days or so. He said he wanted to leave Eugene for Las Vegas to become a professional heckler. Hire himself out to clubs and comedians. He promised he was going to do it next winter."

"Next time Leo went to the comedy club, he walked up to the same comic who had hired him, Buddy whatshisname, and everything was going well between them, and they had some laughs over Leo's performance. As Leo told it, the guy broke off the conversation when Leo mentioned his pay for the night, just disconnected and walked away from Leo."

"Big mistake. Leo was irate about it. To him it was an unforgivable insult. To say he was offended and angry would be

57

an understatement. That night Leo heckled only Buddy and no one else, ambushed him, devastated him. I filmed it. Leo heckled the guy off the stage, practically in tears. It was so bad the club owner banned Leo. The bouncer held him against a wall and took his picture. Leo's photo was passed around to the other comedy club owners in Oregon. 'Beware of Leo.' He was real proud of that."

Taylor paused, a look of awe in his eyes. "He delighted in creating bizarre situations. He loved going to Dr. Ernie so he could torment him. He got a kick out of Dr. Ernie. He called him his all-time favorite counselor."

He and Robert exchanged glances.

"Fucking Leo."

Out in his car, Babe pulled up YouTube. He found the clips of Leo heckling amateur comics at The Comedy Palace in Portland. He was repulsed and amused. Leo was a natural. A shallow soul-sucking glitz town like Vegas would have been perfect.

His phone rang:

"Hello?"

"Yes, Mr. Jackson? We have a problem with the repair you did on the back steps last year. All the cement is falling apart after the winter we had, and Mildred and I like if you could come by and address this little problem. Can you do that for us?"

"I'm sorry, you have the wrong number. This is Babe Hathaway, private investigator. You better check your listing for the correct number."

"Don't try to dodge me, Charlie Jackson. I know your voice and I know where you live. I'm gonna talk to my lawyer. This is my last attempt to settle this. This isn't fair and you're gonna hear about it."

The caller hung up.

Memo: call Lars regarding his used phone.

Chapter 16

"The doctor will see you now."

Babe stood and walked down the hall toward the small red door. He had spent twenty minutes in the waiting room leafing through an odd assortment of magazines, from *Highlights* for kids, to *Maxim* and *Playboy*, for adults. Behind the receptionist was a wall clock the size of the front of a car. The walls were covered with a collage of horses. They all seemed to be smiling.

The receptionist pointed down the hall.

"It's straight ahead."

Babe turned to say thank you. The receptionist, who had stood from her desk and come around to guide him, was less than four feet tall.

"Alright, thank you."

Babe reached the door and entered Dr. Ernie's office. The floor was overly plush, the lighting was set up so that Babe could not see the doctor's face. There were footlights that shone on art objects throughout the room: a vase on a pedestal, a stark violent red painting with expressionistic sensibilities, and a neo-pop sculpture of a child's teddy bear that had been dipped in a brown saucy substance and seemed to be forever ready to continue dripping, the bear's head turned sadly away from the light. The room was otherwise dark.

"Dr. Ernie?" Babe groped forward to the dark desk area and reached out his hand into the area where he expected the doctor to be seated, behind the desk.

"Yes, please sit? Make yourself comfortable."

"Thanks for letting me come to speak with you."

"That's what I'm here for. I'm keeping it a bit dark in here for the moment so that you can relax. You are likely tense. That's normal at first. Take a deep breath and let it out."

"I'm not here to talk about me."

"That's very common. It's okay to refer to certain experiences as if they have happened to a friend, at least at first. It sometimes helps at the beginning. It allows some distance, especially when trauma is involved. So please go on, speak whatever way is most comfortable."

"I'm not sure you understand. I want to talk about Leo Laum. I've been hired by his family to investigate his death. They're not happy about how the police are handling it. Can you help me?"

From the dark, nothing but silence for a moment and then: "Leo Laum!" Dr. Ernie expelled his name with disdain and pounded the desk once as he said it.

"Stinker," the word hissed out under his breath with real disgust.

"What did you say your name was?" Doctor Ernie switched on a small desk lamp and looked down at his appointment pad.

"Babe Hathaway."

"For god sakes, you're not my 10 o'clock appointment. Please leave now. If you want to talk about Leo Laum we can meet elsewhere. Not during business hours. This is my life's work!"

Chapter 17

Babe went home and booted up his laptop. Dr. Ernie was a suspect at this point. The doctor was pissed at Leo. He went to Google and searched for Dr. Ernie. What came up was a set of instructional sex videos available in live streaming, DVD or VHS format.

VHS ? Who used VHS anymore?

Babe ordered online and streamed it on his computer. The doctor was featured throughout and talked incessantly. He was much younger. His hair was cut in a droopy cap of hair as if it were a toupee. He stood at a lectern and chatted about the function of satisfaction. It was boring. He pointed to rudimentary illustrations on the blackboard behind him that showed how the nerves worked.

After fast-forwarding through the first part, Babe came to what was called, "Time to play." Babe expected that it would be a fun romp. Instead, Dr. Ernie talked about the importance of the mouth in sexuality and the development of the child into adulthood by passing through a prolonged oral stage that never quite leaves the adult repertoire.

It was briefly interesting and thought-provoking for Babe, who was interested in the growth of the human psyche. The lecture changed direction and focused on oral hygiene only, throughout the third and final disc. Babe was baffled and bored. He could not understand why Dr. Ernie would be so obsessed with the mouth.

Babe needed more information, something that could conclusively eliminate Dr. Ernie or support further suspicion. Could this man be the killer? Hiding in plain sight? The Google sites referred to his lovely new office. Babe had to call Lars to get some real information, and find out why he was getting a phone call for some guy named Charlie Jackson.

Chapter 18

Babe looked at the clock, it was late morning. He went to the fridge for a snack. As he sat munching, he felt frustrated by the lack of progress on the case. When he finished, he took out his new, Lars-modified, used iPhone.

No return phone call from Lars yet. Typical. I have to call him about the phone.

Babe needed to take a little break so he called Pat O'Leery, his "surveillance expert," drummer friend, and sometime employee to chat and say howdy. Carl invited him to a jam at his friend Jimmy LeBaron's farm outside the city. It was an event Babe needed for his sanity.

Babe checked his expenses and bills and realized his initial retainer was nearly gone. He had to ask for more money. Part of him hoped that Ellen Madsen would call it off, that he would be free from the hustle for money. Poverty had its benefits: he was beholden to no one. Despite his desire for complete freedom, Babe picked up the phone.

"Ellen, this is Babe Hathaway."

"Yes?" Her voice sounded suspicious.

"Sorry to say I have nothing concrete to report so far. I met Leo's immediate family. I visited with Leo's two remaining roommates as well. Both roommates were at home the night he was killed, and the other roommate was back in Connecticut."

"You mean Tim?"

"Yes. Tim Hindler. You knew him? I'm interested in him." Babe paused. "You know Leo tormented him before Tim fled? Leo enjoyed it."

Ellen avoided answering. "I met Tim months ago, when they moved into the quad. You know Tim is a very promising violinist, considered one of the top talents in the country. I hope he gets back on his feet."

She took a moment. Babe could hear her breathe deeply on the phone.

"After the funeral, his roommate, Robert Evans, told me about Leo's horseplay."

"Horseplay? It was torture," Babe replied, with too much heat. "Weren't you shocked when you heard about it?"

"Shocked? No, of course not, Leo was a joker," she shot back. "I wish I had known it had gotten out of hand. I would have stepped in. I'm not like his family. Don't paint me into the same picture as the Laums. My sister married into that mess, not me. She's been changed by it."

As she spoke, her voice rose and became a shrill snarl, like a wounded raccoon backed into a corner. Babe realized he had touched a nerve. She was just getting warmed up.

"I have spent tens of thousands on therapy, and one thing I am clear on: I am not a Laum! You hear me?"

This was not going well. Babe decided to change the subject.

"Believe me Ellen; it's clear that you are not a Laum. Ellen, I never said you were, and I never thought that for a minute. The reason I called is . . . "

"YOU ARE GODDAMMED RIGHT I'M NOT A FUCKING LAUM!"

An uncomfortable silence set in. Babe took a deep breath. He wondered if she had another torrent of anger to let loose.

He closed his eyes and drifted into a theatrical meditation in which he imagined that this interaction was part of a play. He and Ellen were on stage. He saw himself as confident and capable to play his part correctly, able to improvise perfectly, and impress the audience. He would be able to move the story along smoothly. He breathed deeply and slowly.

The question was: what would be the correct part to play? Is this the moment to play the passive/submissive? The counterpuncher? The therapist? The understanding husband?

He decided to try businessman and be clear and unemotional.

"Ellen, the reason I called . . . "

"I am not my sister," she whimpered.

"I know, I know. I'm sorry. Look, I called because I have your invoice prepared."

"Oh I see. I get it. Yeah, I get it." She sniffed with a combination of scorn and satisfaction. "You're on a collection run. You haven't found anything, but you need more money."

Babe closed his eyes and focused on being present. She is playing the domineering, hurt, blaming woman.

Hold your ground.

"Yes, I am calling to let you know that I spent a lot of time at the Laums, and with the police, with the roommates and with Dr. Ernie."

"Maybe if you spent more time detecting and less time cooking inedible meals for Dory and Peter, I wouldn't be headed for the poor house. I heard about that! I'm not paying for any of that food."

"Ellen, that's not a problem, right now I need $5,000 to continue, and I may need more later on. I realize this is a big commitment on your part. Please consider if you want to continue. It is a big, confusing case. It's not simple and will take some time."

She didn't answer for a long time.

"Well, let's see." Her voice was now sweet.

"I will pay the $5,000."

Damn! I was almost free. I should have asked for $10,000.

"I want to hire you for a different job as well."

"What kind of job?"

"Catering and directing a private birthday dinner party at my house."

"You want me to cater an event?"

"I will pay you $3,000 for yourself, plus expenses for this party. It is very important."

Babe saw the money piling up in his bank account, and his bills going down. Babe took notes about the scope of the party, the kind of food, and the number of attendees, to get an overview of the task at hand. By the end of the conversation, she was calm.

"I want you to present scenes and songs. You choose the scenes and songs."

"Well, I don't know . . . "

"Please don't refuse my request. If you do, I will assume you no longer want me to honor Leo, in which case I will end the investigation as well. This is all being done to honor poor Leo." Babe could see her lips quivering briefly. She spoke again, this time in full voice.

"I know you need this money. Everyone in town knows your precarious finances, Babe. It's not a secret that you're hanging on by a thread. You can go only so far on good looks and credit cards. Is it yes or no, Babe?"

Babe didn't answer. It was a deliberate pause. When someone was exerting control, Babe stopped in silence. It allowed for a moment of space to let the energy subside.

Ellen's firm resolve broke. She began breathing heavily and cried. In a moment she was sobbing loudly into the phone. Babe put the phone away from his ear. She was crying hard. It went on and on. He put the phone on the table, sat back in his chair.

He sighed, and picked up the phone. Over her loud sobs he shouted "I'll do it."

She stopped immediately, suddenly calm.

"I will send your check today. Call me tomorrow and we will discuss any and all further details of the dinner party. You can tell me your ideas for a menu. Good bye." She hung up.

Scenes and songs?

Chapter 19

Babe walked to the window and looked out. He gazed idly over the treetops and drifted in reverie.

I have to eliminate suspects. I want to be done with this. I need information.

Somewhere between the annoying hustle to make ends meet and the joys of performance, Babe found adequate motivation to continue forward. He phoned Lars Boothe. Lars could get him information that was not readily available in the public domain.

"Lars. Hey. How're you doing?"

"The Babester, Umm, same-same, laying low . . . What's up?"

"I need to use your services."

"I have time this afternoon after the Tokyo exchange closes. Then I'm free. Just send me a quick, text of the names, and I'll get started. Why don't you come on up the mountain again? Ring me when you get to the lower gate, and I'll get you past the Dobermans."

"They were in cages just the other day."

"My neighbor's having a dispute with a biker and he's feeling paranoid. He asked that I let Betsy and Clyde loose inside the fence. It makes him feel safer."

"I'm on my way. You can bill me for this."

"Babe, I don't need your money for this. I need some food. How about you bring me gazpacho, a baguette, curried chicken salad, a raspberry torte and a side order of Miley Cyrus."

"Remind me to talk to you about the phone, Lars. I'm getting some calls to the previous owner or so it seems."

"Oh that. Well, I may not be able to fix that. It comes with the territory. Sorry."

Babe hung up and sent a text containing the names he wanted investigated, and walked out to his car. Storm clouds were moving in low and fast from the south west, not raining yet, probably soon. He drove downtown, and noticed people scurrying in their raincoats, ready for any weather. *God, I love this town.* Babe swung past a deli and picked up lunch.

As he drove west, food bags next to him on the passenger seat, he thought about Lars. The man sounded pretty upbeat today. He tended to be gloomy, sitting up there alone with all that electronic gear.

Years back Lars had hired Babe to follow his soon to be ex-wife. They were separated, and his wife had custody of their child for the time being. Babe hired Pat O'Leery to spy. It had been a rocky separation, a devastating custody negotiation and divorce. Lars ended up with a restraining order against him. His ex turned their six-year old daughter against him. A painful year later, Lars gave up the fight and the drama subsided.

Soon after the divorce, Lars moved to a quiet, isolated place up a steep gravel road on a nearby hill. Since moving, he had flourished financially. Lars enjoyed his solitude. He came down the hill for provisions, otherwise he stayed home.

Babe headed west until the turnoff. When he got to Lars' fence, he phoned. Two Doberman Pinschers leapt at the fence, furiously barking and slavering. Babe noticed their tails wagging. Nice act guys. Probably lick someone to death.

A serious face-licking ensued when Lars emerged from his truck and opened the gate. Babe took a running start up the hill, spinning gravel around the curves until he got to the parking lot: a crude pad bulldozed out of the red dirt side of the hill. Giant firs shaded everything. Lars' truck came roaring up moments later. Babe handed Lars the groceries.

Babe admired Lars' house: a 50-foot diameter, wooden, yurt-like structure with a giant skylight over the center. It was connected to smaller yurts by enclosed hallways. Lars had designed and built it as a form of divorce therapy. He kept improving it. Now there were flower boxes. The place looked downright homey for a bachelor pad. Babe was glad.

Lars was more at home with computer hacking and futures trading than ordinary social situations. After his restraining order debacle, Lars trusted Babe, and they became friends.

Lars was heavyset, with a bushy red beard and skin so red it looked as if it had been abraded. His dark-framed glasses accentuated the redness. He wore Carhart canvas trousers, a logger's striped shirt and suspenders.

Lars put the food in the kitchen. They prepared two plates of food and went down a hallway into the office yurt to eat. A satellite dish stood outside the window. The walls and desks were covered with computer gear. Screens streamed world financial information. Lars hit a button and the screens changed to the ocean, gentle waves breaking against palm tree lined beaches.

"I like the kill dogs, Lars, real frightening."

"The Hollywood reputation of Dobermans seems to be enough of a deterrent. I have a hard time getting them out of my truck. The truth is, nobody comes up that road who I don't know anyhow."

"Is that live?" Babe pointed to one of the screens.

"Yeah, Costa Rica. Here, check this one out." He pressed some keys and the screens showed the earth. "This is live from the space station. Pretty cool, eh?"

"Yeah. Leave that one up."

Lars tore hungrily at the food. "Good, good."

They ate in silence. They went back for seconds.

"Find anything out?" asked Babe as he sat back down in the office.

Lars handed Babe a flash drive.

Babe took it. He knew never to ask how Lars' had acquired the data.

Lars took a chunk of baguette and dipped it in the gazpacho.

"That's everything I could get: the family, Dr. Ernie, Robert, Taylor, and Tim, the roommates. Anybody else? I can get it pretty quick." Lars wiped his lips on a napkin and continued.

"You know, Babe, I saw this on the news. Cops said it was a hit and run. Did you check out the actors and the theater crew? Maybe someone got angry? That's got to be a possibility. I took a look at a couple of the YouTube clips about Leo heckling some comedians. Real savage stuff, the audience was laughing like crazy. Made me squirm, guy had talent. Maybe he did that heckling routine to a touchy actor at the theater?"

"I'm heading over to the theater tomorrow. I'll have some names for you after that. But for now, I need to focus on the alibis of the family, the roommates and Dr. Ernie."

"That's what I expected." Lars wiped his hands on the napkin and motioned for Babe to hand back the flash drive. Lars plugged it in, and pulled up a file. He pointed at the screen.

"Mostly no alibis popped out of the data for anybody, except . . . voilà, a suspect."

Babe leaned into the screen. It showed an airline ticket itinerary, Hartford to Seattle. The departure and return dates surrounding the time of the murder. The passenger: Timothy Hindler.

Babe stood up. He pursed his lips and shook his head.

"Here's something else." Lars brought up an invoice, a rental car.

"This could be the murder vehicle, could be evidence left on it."

"Good work." Babe thought of something. "How many miles did he put on that vehicle."

"I thought of that too. But so far I haven't been able to get past the firewall and get any specific vehicle data to check the mileage."

Babe considered this, while he ate a forkful of curried chicken salad. "That still might not prove anything. He could have rented a car, paid cash."

Lars shook his head. He started flipping through invoices.

"Anything is possible. But why have all these other bills on his credit card, out in the open. Here's a motel receipt; here's a meal at the Evergreen College student union."

"He's establishing an alibi."

"There's information on Dr. Ernie in there. No alibi and no motive, but the guy is unlicensed as a counselor. He used to be a dentist."

"Dentist?"

"Yeah. Did you know dentists have the highest suicide rate of any professional?"

"I never thought about it," said Babe.

"Maybe it's from looking down into all those mouths. When you think of it, looking at a mouthful of unbrushed, rotting teeth, whew! I couldn't do it."

Lars extracted the flash drive and handed it to Babe. The view on the screens went back to the view from the space station. The sun was just coming up over Australia; large cloud banks covered the equator.

"That is why you private dicks get the big money."

Babe stood to leave. "You seem happy, Lars."

"First visitation with my kid in a year, supervised, but still, I saw her, even though her mother and her new boyfriend were right there the whole time. I have no other good options, and I'm done fighting. I just want to spend time with my kid."

"Good for you," said Babe as he opened the front door.

"I'll call as soon as I find out more on the car. I'll follow you down to lock the gate. "

Chapter 20

Dr. Ernie agreed to meet at a small restaurant downtown. Babe got a table in the front window and saw the doctor as he approached. Standing to greet him, Babe put out his hand.

"Sorry to have disturbed you during your practice. I am grateful you are willing to take the time to meet with me."

"Certainly." He nodded and sat down. He was dressed in loose fitting pants and a white shirt. His hair was clearly false, the color of his wig and his real hair were vastly different and no effort had been made to create an artful transition of color and texture.

As an actor, Babe noticed the way people presented themselves. Dr. Ernie tended to lean forward. He was about 5 foot 10. He had a pair of glasses that he put on and took off frequently.

"Cup of coffee? Something to eat?"

"I'm eating and you're paying. How's that?"

"That's fine with me." Babe handed the doctor a menu and put down the folder that Lars had given him.

After a quick perusal of the menu, he stated, "I'm ready to order, call her over."

Babe noted his demanding, unsociable manner. Babe leaned back and turned to look for the waitress. He found her and waved. She came right over.

"I'm having the penne noodles with vodka sauce and swordfish. I will be having the small arugula salad with vinaigrette, and an iced tea, thank you."

"And you sir? What would you like? By the way my husband and I, we watch your show all the time. All the food looks so good. He gave me your cook book last year for Xmas." She giggled and blushed.

"I'm glad you like the show. What's fresh today?"

"I would recommend the mussels marinara and a side of cooked escarole in garlic and oil."

"Sounds great, and I'll have an iced tea too."

The waitress turned and left.

"Are you famous?" The doctor asked.

"Local celebrity, a TV cooking show and I do local theater too. Right now I'm working as a PI to look into a problem the police can't or won't deal with."

Dr. Ernie leaned over the table. He seemed to be sniffing Babe and looking at his teeth at the same time. There was a slight grimace on his face while he did so.

"So you used to be a dentist. Retired?" Babe knew from Lars' dossier that there had been some unaccountability in his dental practice that moved him swiftly in the direction of quitting.

"Mr. Hathaway, there are some events in our professional lives that we cannot control. We have to acknowledge them and move on."

Dr. Ernie leaned back in his chair, looked up at the ceiling and put the tips of his fingers to his nose and sniffed them. His eyelids closed slightly as he did so. Babe thought Dr. Ernie was experiencing some kind of euphoria caused by the aroma of his fingers.

"What about Leo Laum? He's gone. The police are doing nothing about it?"

"Leo, yellow incisors, tart, constantly changing breath, always worse. That bastard knew immediately I was sensitive to smell and he taunted me." He turned and shook his head, his clenched jaw showed anger, hostility. This guy disliked Leo intensely.

"So you didn't like him?"

At this question, the doctor leaned back. Babe, following protocol based on theatrical postures and improv principles, leaned forward across the table to maintain nearness. Dr. Ernie relaxed and shook his head.

"He deliberately ate strong-smelling foods just before coming into the office. Salami with onions and garlic pickles, followed by belching deep from his gullet. It was wretched. Other times he would drink dark coffee and smoke Turkish cigarettes before coming for his session. He would sit near the desk and exhale the pungent smell of a rotting gut; it was the smell of stagnant bowels coming up the wrong way combined with bad gums. Oh, how I hated my sessions with him."

"Why didn't you fire him? Was he making progress?"

"To be frank, his folks paid the bill on time and I needed the money. After the dental business folded, and by the way, the court case was based solely on conjecture—I never touched her. We settled out of court, the malpractice insurance wouldn't cover it either, those fucks. I should have had someone in the room with me every time. Sure I got close to her, but I just wanted to smell her breath. It's a valid part of my diagnosis. She didn't understand and neither did her mother." He hissed his way through the explanation, sneering and shaking his head.

Babe thought to himself: this is a guy with a lot of anger and boundary issues. He might be the one.

The meal came. It was above average. A meal like this is usually rated as "Pretty good." The "Not bad" category usually meant you wouldn't get sick from it.

"Do you like horses, Babe?"

Babe was perplexed.

"I don't know much about them."

Dr. Ernie relaxed and spoke with great enthusiasm.

"I adore them. I have two mini horses in a small stable behind my house. I would never give up my gentleman's farm or my beautiful little horses."

He leaned forward, and absent-mindedly sniffed the air close to Babe's mouth. Babe quickly leaned back.

Dr. Ernie is a creep.

Dr. Ernie smiled and exhaled.

"Not bad. Your front teeth and incisors are quite balanced with a modest overbite, and you certainly have good gum cleaning habits. Stay away from the whitener though . . . Where was I? Oh, yes, horses. The horse is a lovely animal, big lovely teeth, and their breath is sweet like the hay and grass they chew all day. No fats, no decomposing proteins to promote foul fermentation like humans. No odd animal fats to lodge in the back of the mouth or cause eructation, no great clouds of effluvia, steamy and rife with sulfurous compounds. The mouth is similar to the anus if not taken care of well."

As he talked, he ate mouthfuls of food and nodded his head from side to side. It was as if he were singing and reciting. He returned again to the horse.

"The equine system is so efficient, elegant and simple. There's no gall bladder, you see. No unreliable fat breakdown, no triggered liver enzymes. It's all so simple, just grass, oats, hay. Very clean. And if you get to know them, they are happy to let you get close and sniff their chlorophyll-fresh breath. I love my horses."

"Do you ride?" asked Babe.

"Just a trot around my track now and then, but I keep them as companions and to sniff their breath. It calms me. It takes me to my quiet spot."

Oh Boy!

"What about Leo, Dr. Ernie? Who might have killed him?"

"I guess you think I did it."

"Did you?"

"It was an accident! Clearly an accident. No one killed that awful schmuck. Don't waste your time. Police said it was a hit and run. Why muck around with it any longer? Trying to make a few extra bucks, are you? I can understand that. But why prolong the agony of his parents, I say. He's already buried. Leave his stinky asshole mouth in the ground."

Babe saw that Dr. Ernie was half out of his chair, nearly ready to storm out.

"Okay. Sit down, please. I'm trying to get some closure for the family on this, and there are some avenues that haven't been addressed."

"Well make it snappy, Hathaway. Stringing them along for a pay check is immoral, isn't it? On the other hand, if you want to buy me lunch again, I am always happy to go. In fact, there is a new place downtown I'd like to try. Maybe you have more questions that I haven't answered adequately today? What about a dinner? I love Italian food."

74

Babe stood at the end of the meal, after the bill had been paid and extended his hand to Dr. Ernie. Dr. Ernie was still deep into his second dessert.

"I must run. I have another appointment and must not be late. Thank you for your time."

"Let me know about dinner." Dr. Ernie looked up from the chocolate mousse his lips smeared, his wig now slightly to the side of his head from his rapturous head nodding.

As Babe walked away, Dr. Ernie called after him: "I invite you to come to my farm and meet my horses. Their breath is ambrosial!"

Chapter 21

Even when she was a wearing a lab coat and large black rimmed glasses, Terri Lemon was a knockout. Her straight black hair and bright white teeth glowed. Her smile was like the sun. Her solid shoulders and upright carriage told the story of an extremely fit athlete. In fact, she qualified for Olympic javelin and would have gone if it weren't for the accidental death of both her parents in a car crash. It hit her hard. All that was left for her was to pick up the pieces and take care of her little sister, a punky high schooler at the time.

Babe half lifted out of his seat and waved to her. Terri grinned and made her way across the room like Lady Liberty passing between the small islands off the coast of New Jersey.

"Terri, it's been too long." He stood and gave her a big hug.

"Three months. I know because the season has changed." She shook her head and sat down.

The waitress came and dropped off glasses of water. But she didn't leave. She stared at Terri intensely. It was all she could do. Absently, she stepped on Babe's foot and apologized. Such was the effect Terri had on those in her presence. Babe was used to it.

It was hard at first to accept that she was "playing for the other team." That's how she explained it when they first met at a bar by chance several years ago. They had both been stood up by dates and they waited, wounded, sipping drinks and making small talk. The conversation went on into the night and they remained friends since.

They ordered food and settled in. Terri worked as a forensic scientist for the Oregon State Police, and she talked about her latest case, a car accident. The blood types found in the car showed there was at least one other person in the car, a person who fled the scene, leaving the driver dying behind the wheel.

"Terri, I've been working on that hit and run downtown. The guy was on his bike, and he may have been deliberately run over. My client thinks her nephew was singled out and brutally executed that night. I can't figure it out. So far, I'm finding everyone had a love/hate relationship with him: a real wise guy, annoying, pulled a lot of practical jokes, but at the same time he loved to party and wanted his peeps to have a great time."

"Yeah, I read about it, but the cops didn't send anything to us on it. Is there any blood on the tires or tire marks that I can run through the lab? Fingerprints, paint spots, anything? If you find even a ghost of something I can run it through the equipment lab. We can detect the smell of shampoo on a pillow, anything, Babe."

"There's nothing. No car, no witnesses, the cops have given up. The guy's aunt hired me to find out who did it. She thinks Leo was killed, that's all I've got." Babe shook his head and played with the straw in his iced tea.

"I'm sorry Babe. Shit. Hey, it's spring, let's have a party. Are you game?"

"Count me in Terri. I could use a good party."

Chapter 22

Babe dialed his cell phone, Terri picked up.

"Terri, I just talked to the police about Leo's case. They have a photo of a tire mark. I'll bring it to you. I also have a possible lead on a rental car. If the two tires are a match we could have our killer."

"Did they say they had a sample of the tread rubber? One particle of it and we could take the investigation to the next level. Remember, we have very sensitive equipment here. The cops in this town are so inept, especially the ones who arrive first on the scene. I'm thinking of giving a class for cops on state-of-the-art evidence collection. Cases can be broken in minutes using far less information than what used to be required."

Terri swung out into details about her analytical machines and how they worked. It was like going to a science fair and listening to an excited teenager.

"Terri, maybe you can speak to the cops. The detective I spoke to wanted nothing to do with me."

"Let me guess: It was Carenza, right? You can't talk to him. He's fucked up, always angry. See if you can find Errol Smith, mellow detective, doesn't take himself seriously. I think he was a marine or Special Forces. To him, the crime here in town is like eating cold cereal compared to what he's been through. The trouble is he works under Carenza. He is a big soft pretzel fan, so if you go see him, don't go empty handed."

"Soft pretzels it shall be. Thanks, Terri. I'm still thinking about what to cook for our party."

"Don't think too long."

Chapter 23

It was jam night. Babe looked forward to falling into an unconscious creative zone with his fellow groove-makers. He arrived at Jimmy LeBaron's quiet farm west of Eugene just before sunset. As he pulled into the parking area in front of the old barn, his phone rang.

"Hi Charlie," said a quavering voice. "This is Erma Phelps. I need your help. My toilet won't stop running. Can you come over please?"

"I'm sorry, I am not Charlie Jackson."

"But you did such a good job installing my gas stove."

"I'm not Charlie Jackson. I didn't install your stove."

"But you answered Charlie's phone, so you have to fix the toilet."

"Since when . . . Look, that's not the business I am in. I'm busy now."

"What is your business? What are you so busy doing?"

"That's none of your business."

"Don't get huffy with me, young man!"

"Sorry. I have to go. Good bye."

Damn you Lars.

The old fruit-drying shed, now the jam space, was already bumping out a rhythm into the young night. No one living nearby would hear a bit of it. Babe could feel the drums and bass in his chest as he approached. He needed to have a word with O'Leery, the drummer, and he needed to get into the groove and surrender.

As soon as he entered he was handed a lit pipe of medical grade cannabis. Babe smiled and sucked in the gentle unguent.

Babe saw Pat O'Leery, the skinny, perpetually nervous drummer. Pat was Babe's part-time surveillance guy. Pat nodded. Babe nodded his chin at Pat.

"See me afterwards. I have a job for you."

"Babe, I bought a tiny digital spy camera, it can be concealed anywhere."

Pat was a former meth addict, who had given up his addiction though remained scarred and agitated from the experience. He was either all on – or all off. When he took the bit between his teeth on anything, he tended toward overdoing it. Purchasing a spy camera for possible use on one of his infrequent surveillance jobs was overkill. Babe made a mental note to direct him about the limits of the surveillance task at hand, and to influence Pat to return the camera and get his money back.

In a few minutes, after brief greetings, everyone who was not already playing had moved to their instruments and began noodling. There were four saxophones tonight, a real power horn section. Everyone knew each other and played well together.

"What do you want to play?" asked Babe, sitting at his keyboard.

Everyone looked at each other.

"Try this to get us started," O'Leery announced. He began a rhythm and the bass player got into it with him. Babe began hitting big chords with his left hand and the pace developed. After a few dozen bars, the others joined in. The groove developed, and it built and grew into a stirring modal improv. Then the sax section began playing a funky, gospel riff that others picked up and the improvisation morphed into "Mercy, Mercy," a Joe Zawinul tune.

Babe instantly felt relief. He felt lucky to be alive. The stress slipped away. All of the dysfunctional people faded away. They couldn't touch him here. The music was medicine for the soul.

The jam burned for 4 intense hours, changing along the way. They played some originals, some jazz standards and one more extended improvisation. Along the way Babe sang 'How high the Moon', and 'It don't mean a thing if it ain't got that swing.' It was a magical evening of musical connection. Everyone felt it.

Afterwards, Babe went outside on the porch and waited for Pat. There was a light drizzle, and the temperature was almost 50 degrees. After a cold winter a warmer night felt great. The musicians left, except for Pat. Pat came out, carrying his drum stick case.

"So what is this surveillance case you have for me? I'm ready to go."

"Great Pat, I'm glad you're ready to go. I don't need pictures this time. Just stay back. Take notes. Don't confront anyone. I do not—*under any circumstances*—want you to be seen or discovered."

"You know me, man. I can hide, blend, be invisible."

Pat was good, but Babe knew he had to put some boundaries in place, to tamp down Pat's edgy enthusiasm.

Babe explained that he wanted Pat to conduct surveillance on the Laum Family first, then the roommates and finally Dr. Ernie.

"I'll start tonight."

"It's 11:30, Pat. You don't have to start tonight."

"But I want to."

Babe didn't see any reason to argue. He gave Pat the addresses.

"Pat, can you get back your money on that camera?" Pat was always one step away from being broke or homeless. That was one of the reasons Babe hired him. Pat was good-hearted and had a great sense of humor. He knew he was unbalanced and fortunately could laugh at himself and his frequent misadventures. He told his personal stories with humor and without embarrassment. Babe admired the way he coped with his imbalance. Babe remembered the old joke: what do you call a drummer without a girlfriend? Homeless. Pat was worth helping, one hell of a drummer, and a very loyal, if volatile, friend.

"I like this camera. I'll think about it."

Pat trotted out to his car. Babe wondered what kind of manic trouble Pat would get into. He shook his head.

As Pat drove off, Babe stood in the misty night and felt joy. What a wonderful evening, friends, music . . . *God, I love Oregon,* he thought. Babe stuck his head into the music building to say goodbye. Jimmy, the farm owner and alto saxophonist, was coiling up instrument chords.

"Wait a second, Babe. Can I talk to you a minute?" said Jimmy.

"What's up?"

"You sounded good tonight, Babe."

"Well thanks, you too."

"I want to ask a favor. It's a paying job."

Babe thanked him but explained that he was currently employed and very busy at the moment, and therefore unavailable.

"This won't take but a minute. It's really small. I mean, no time at all."

Babe heard him out.

"Okay, what's up?"

"Well, my wife's brother is a sculptor, his name is Godric Walpole. He's a little quirky, his art is a little weird too, but he's talented, and he has made some sales. He has a niche market. Anyway, this art collector, the winery owner Ernesto Figlio – you've heard of him—met Godric once, at a show in town. Figlio's a big art supporter; he contributes and buys art, all that good stuff. Godric's work was part of the show. So, Figlio goes to the opening, and . . . this is where it gets strange."

"This is a paying job, right?" asked Babe, skeptically.

"Yes, Godric will pay you to confront Figlio, and get him to stop harassing him."

"Why doesn't he call the cops?"

"He tried. They said there was no crime committed."

"You said it won't take much time?"

"Sure. You can go see Godric now. Just go over there. You can't call him, his phone is always off. He sculpts at night and sleeps during the day. I'm sure he's up."

Babe took the address and left, shaking his head, wondering what he was getting into. Ordinarily, he genuinely liked artists, and enjoyed meeting them. An impromptu visit to a sculptor's studio could be fun, but Leo Laum was consuming all of Babe's time, focus, and energy. Despite Leo's toxic exploits, Babe had moments of real curiosity about who may have killed Leo Laum, and why. At other moments, he just wanted it to be over.

Leo was such a creative sadist; there must have been enemies. And then what about old grudges carried by earlier victims? Leo collected victims and relished in their misfortunes. He seemed rabid at times.

So what if Leo was sometimes charming, generous and funny? That doesn't cut it. Leo must have finally paid the price. Babe had a chilling vision. He pulled the car over to the side of the road and put on the emergency brake. He closed his eyes.

Leo's face appeared. It was formed by wisps of smoke in the dark night. Leo was laughing and dead. He was laughing at Babe. His poisoned red eyes were enjoying one more torment from the safety of death. He was tormenting Babe.

Chapter 24

Godric Walpole's home and sculpture studio was a tiny unkempt house that overlooked the hiking trails around The Laurelwood golf course in the South East Eugene hills. Godric didn't open the door when Babe knocked.

"Who's there?" He shouted.

"Jimmy LeBaron said you might need some help dealing with Ernesto Figlio." Babe hollered.

The door swung open, and a heavyset man wearing a clay crusted apron, motioned Babe inside. Flecks of clay had dried in his mop of curly dark brown hair. His hands and lower arms were covered in wet clay.

"I won't shake your hand."

They walked back to the studio. Babe heard classical music.

Babe stopped at the door. He was amazed by what he saw. There were hundreds of little clay baby shoes everywhere. Every shelf, every table was stacked with finished and unfinished clay baby shoes. They were in all sizes, all colors, from white porcelain to black enamel, and every color in between. Cardboard boxes and mailing supplies took up one corner, but the rest of the room was devoted to baby shoes. A door was open to a second room that held fine art pieces.

"Let me turn off the music. Grab a chair."

"The music is fine." Babe brushed clay dust off a stool, and sat next to a table, covered with itty, bitty, thimble sized porcelain baby shoes, laces painted on in blue and pink.

Godric leaned against another table, where he was working on a huge baby shoe, at least a size 15, fashioning it out of greenish clay.

He pointed at the shoe he was working on: "Special order, going to Taiwan. More and more of my business is now special order. Those little ones next to you are favored by collectors of Hummel figures."

"I see. Looks like you're busy."

"I am. I can afford a car now. I couldn't do that when I did fine art sculptures. Now I can buy food."

"Way to go." A success story in the art community was always welcome news.

"You specialize in little shoes."

"Baby shoes in particular. People buy them from my website, or send me their kid's or grandkid's baby shoes, and I make a beautiful replica in a variety of colors. I send it out in a pretty box, with a card, and orders keep coming in."

Babe suddenly felt tired. He wanted to get down to business and go home. He opened his notebook.

"Jimmy told me you are having trouble with Ernesto Figlio? I met him once. He seemed like a nice man."

Godric's shoulders slumped.

"What happened?"

"Ernesto was on a panel of judges for a show in Portland. I put some of my old fine art pieces in the show."

"No baby shoes?"

Godric shot an annoyed look at Babe. "Look. I know fine art from craft. This . . . " He pointed at the shoe-filled room . . . "is making a living."

"Sorry, go on."

"I won the show, and sometime during the cocktail party afterwards, I had a brief conversation with Figlio. He congratulated me, praised my work highly. He had an impressive knowledge of modern sculpture. He told me he was a sculptor too, so I invited him to my studio."

Godric paused and let out a breath.

"That was my mistake. I never invite people, even artists, to my studio. This is my sanctuary. Nobody knows about this shoe business. I only sell on the Internet. But there I was, first place ribbon in hand, and the flattery got to me I guess."

"So?"

"When Figlio got here, he asked what these baby shoes were all about. I told him. Then he asked to see my studio, where I do my art. This was the work that he was excited to see. I told him those pieces in the show were the old me, the starving artist.

85

When I told him I had no fine art projects planned at any time, he became irate. He flipped out."

"What did he do?"

"He took it personally for some reason. When I told him I was happy with my life sculpting baby shoes for Internet sales, he got down on his knees and begged me to go back to sculpting fine art. I refused. I thought it was funny at first. Then he got aggressive. He's short and strong. He went from begging me to screaming at me in a couple of seconds. I was shocked. He was telling me that I was wasting my talent, that every second was precious with a talent like mine."

Godric paused.

"Here is what he said, and this is a quote: 'How dare you?'"

Godric said it again, imitating an indignant man, thrusting his chin at Babe.

"How dare you?"

"Figlio is a passionate man, but why about this?" said Babe.

"He ridiculed my little shoes, went on this rant and then he stormed out of my house. All the way to his car, he kept shouting 'how dare you'."

"That's disturbing. I am sorry to hear this."

"It gets worse. That was just the beginning. Two days later, a note was put under my windshield wiper. It showed an angry smiley face and a crude drawing of a gun, with the words 'Bang' under the face."

"You took this to the police, right?"

"Of course. There were no fingerprints, no evidence. They wouldn't do anything, even after I named Figlio. I had no way of proving he was even at my studio. Then I talked to a friend at a local clay studio, and things started making sense. My friend told me that Figlio suffers from extreme artist's block. He has taken every class in sculpture, read every book, has an amazing studio out at his winery, artists-in-residence live there, and he has never produced a single sculpture of his own in thirty years. He would love to make something – anything – but he is paralyzed and can't move forward."

"This is crazy."

"He is angry, and jealous, and he is taking it out on me. I got a second note a couple of weeks later. This one just has a crude drawing of a baby shoe, with flames shooting out of the top. The police sent a car around once a night for two weeks after that. I haven't had any more notes. But I can't sleep well. Can you help me?"

Babe got up, folded his notebook.

"I'll go see Figlio. But first, you have to understand, if I contact him, this becomes a paying job."

"Money is tight right now. After I bought the car, everything is tied up in materials for making the baby shoes. It'll be a couple of months before the cash flow comes around. You know how it is in business."

"I work with artists, how about a trade?"

"Sure. I'd rather trade. Oh, I am so grateful to you, thank you, thank you."

He was nearly in tears.

Babe walked into the second room. There were several very attractive tabletop size sculptures. He could picture one in particular on his living room table.

"How about this one?" He pointed at a graceful abstract piece in muted colors.

Godric came over, motioned Babe out of the room, and quickly closed the door.

The tears and gratitude were gone. "No. Those are not available. Come over here." Babe followed. Godric picked up a thin, gold-colored chain that was strung with several thimble-sized porcelain baby shoes, each one painted in a different muted pastel color.

"Here. This will look splendid hanging on your rear view mirror."

He held it out to Babe.

This is my pay?

Babe reluctantly took the string of shoes, and dropped it into his pocket with a smirk.

He held up a finger. "One visit, that's all I'm going to do for you. I will go see Figlio tomorrow, then it's over."

"Oh, thank you. You are a treasure. You know, in the arts community, you have such a good reputation."

For being a chump.

In his Dodge Dart, he took the chain of baby shoes and put it on his rear view mirror. It looked stupid.

Chapter 25

While Babe was getting paid in porcelain baby shoes, Pat O'Leery was in his car down the street from the Laum residence, fiddling with his new spy camera. Despite the fact that Babe did not ask for pictures, Pat was excited to use his camera. The buttons were small, and Pat kept pressing the wrong ones. The screen would go blank, or the camera would turn itself off, or it would take a flash picture of the floor of the car. Slowly, he stumbled through figuring out how the damn thing worked.

Maybe Babe's right, maybe I should return it.

It was perfectly quiet in the Eugene hills. The streets were wet and it was 55 degrees. Low clouds hung overhead.

Pat was dressed in black. He closed the door silently and tread quietly in the shadows toward the Laum residence. He saw a light coming around the curtains of one ground floor window, indicating that somebody might be awake. In a few minutes his eyes adjusted to the dark. He stopped at the house next to the Laums and hid behind a tree to scope out the front yard: good cover, lots of trees, shrubs, no gate into the backyard and three cars in the driveway.

He waited ten minutes. He saw the light in a ground floor room flicker once, as somebody inside moved around. He decided to get closer, get the lay of the land. He stepped behind a rhododendron bush in the Laum front yard and waited. He could see a way to get from the bush to a tree and then into the back yard.

He moved to the tree near the window. A car drove down the street, and he dropped down. After the car passed, he moved closer to the window. There was just a crack of light. He moved past the window and took ten slow steps down the walkway into the back yard. It was perfectly quiet and very dark. He could barely see as he slowly shuffled in the grass. His foot hit a metal object and he stopped. He couldn't identify the object. He decided to turn back, and slowly retraced his steps.

As he began walking toward the road, he felt a gun barrel in his ear.

"On your knees, hands on your head or I will blow your head off." It was a woman's voice.

For a second he felt like running, but the gun pushed harder. Pat fell to his knees. Hope left him. He was already a convicted felon, and he had a vision of prison.

"Keep your hands on your head. Stand up."

One hand patted him down. The gun hand moved. She removed his phone and keys

"What's this? Pervert camera?" She held the spy camera.

"Follow me. Be quiet." She led him through a side door into the garage. She turned on the light. Pat saw an attractive dark haired woman in her thirties, dressed in a black leather jumpsuit, holding a revolver: Susie Laum, exactly as Babe had described her.

She put her finger to her lips, and motioned him down a dark hallway to a room where the light was on. Pat walked inside. She closed the door behind him and motioned him to sit on the bed. She kept the gun trained on his stomach.

"Take a look, idiot."

She moved the mouse on her computer and the screen showed the entire yard clearly lit by infrared.

"Did you really think there wasn't security? I could shoot you. Maybe I will. I saw you when you were standing behind the Miller's tree. In fact, here is the entire tape. She pressed a key and a video came up. It was Pat moving about the yard.

"Here's what I will say. You crept up on our house. You spied into my bedroom, you came in to our back yard and you opened my window. I was terrified. You threatened my life, so I shot you. It's all on the computer, except me shooting you." She waved the gun at him. "Who are you? Give me your wallet?" He handed her the wallet.

"Pat O'Leery."

"Let's see who you really are. She put the gun down, and typed on the computer. She got Pat's full name, and address.

"Bingo, there you are. Hmmm. Let's see. One meth arrest, 90 days in jail, some juvenile records that I can't see. What was your juvenile arrest for?"

"Uh, it was pot." This was a lie. Actually he got caught, at age 12, trespassing outside several houses at night. Two of the neighbors set up a trap, and caught him. One of the men had daughters and beat him up pretty bad. He went to court, then counseling, then probation. He knew he was wrong, but after all these years he still liked to sneak. It wasn't sexual. He got a rush going into places where he shouldn't be.

"What should I do with you? You're too ugly to fuck."

She looked at the camera.

"And here is your pervert camera. Were you going to try to get pictures of me naked? Susie said.

"No. No."

"Yeah right." She moved the buttons on the camera, and quickly got it working.

She held it in her hand for a minute, thinking. Then she picked up the pistol, went over to the window and opened it.

"Climb out the window and stand there. And if you run, I will shoot you in the back."

Pat climbed out the window.

"Good. Now take this camera, and take a picture of me."

"What? I wasn't going to take pictures of you."

"What does a pervert do with a camera except take naked pictures of innocent women? Take my picture!"

Pat took the camera. Susie put the gun under a pillow. Pat held the camera to his eye.

"Wait." She turned sideways, and unzipped her leather suit, exposing her bra.

"Now, take the picture."

He took the picture.

"Now take one from the other side."

He took the picture.

"Give me the camera and climb back in."

Pat climbed inside. She shut the window and drew the drapes. She pointed the camera at him.

"I now have everything I need to send you to prison, peeping Tom. Now tell me why you chose our house?

And Pat told her everything. He told her that Babe hired him. He told her he was to watch the Laums, the roommates, and Dr. Ernie.

She sniffed at the name Dr. Ernie.

"Let me think." She drummed the camera on her knee for a long time.

She went over to a dresser and removed a pair of skimpy panties. She balled them up.

"Open your mouth, perv."

She shoved the panties in.

"How would you like to avoid prison, Pat?"

"mmmhummfff"

She held out her hand. "Spit it out."

She threw the panties below the window.

"Now I have your DNA. How would you like to avoid prison?"

"I would."

"Good. Then it is time for this little investigation of Babe Hathaway's to come to an end." She stood and walked over to him, and pushed him.

"From now on, you will report to me on anything you see, and everything you hear from Babe. Ask him questions. Don't come back here. I will call you. If you leave anything out, I will know, and I will turn this camera and the panties over to the police."

"I will do it," said Pat, greatly relieved.

"Oh, and there is one more thing. I want you to tail my aunt, Ellen Madsen. Follow her every day, starting tomorrow. Tell me everything you find out.

Susie opened the window.

"Now get out!"

Driving home, Pat felt a moment of relief at avoiding arrest. He was overcome by the insistent gnawing in the pit of his stomach: he had failed Babe. He had given Babe up to save himself. He betrayed his friend. Babe had told him to lay low and avoid detection. This was far worse.

Chapter 26

"Hi Eamon, it's Babe Hathaway. I hope you don't mind me calling on your cell number rather than the business line. I wanted to make sure I caught you."

"Well I'm home this morning. I work from home sometimes, it makes life easier. I step one foot into the theater and its non-stop questions and hustle. You must be busy too, with your TV shows and all your events."

"Well, I get plenty of time by myself, and it gets kind of quiet. It comes with the territory, busy and in the middle of things, or quiet and alone."

"Yeah, I get lonely too. So what's on your mind, what can I do for you?"

"It's the Laum case. There are many loose ends I need to look into. I need to go through Leo's relationships with the cast and crew at the theater. I want to eliminate them from suspicion, if I can, and I want to do it soon."

"I understand. Well, I have a suggestion, why don't you swing by the house and we can have some alone time, just you and me. We can chat and have a cup of coffee and I can show you the view from my porch on the hill. It is absolutely breathtaking. That way we can visit and shake free of that loneliness and talk, you know, have some man time together. I can stay at home all morning, there's nothing pressing at work. I'm all yours. Whattya say?"

Is he coming on to me?

The cloying tone of Eamon's voice rang a bell. He had heard it before. Babe remembered having an interview at an employment office when he was in his early twenties, trying to make a living while attending casting calls in New York City: One lone guy manning the desk in an office about to close, until Babe showed up. The guy ordered up some coffee and after a long informal conversation, he mentioned that his neighbor often provided sexual favors just for the fun of it. He invited Babe to his house for a meal and some of the neighbor's generosity. After a long subway ride and dinner, the neighbor didn't seem to be home. The employment office guy turned out to be the randy "neighbor" he spoke of, saying that he would gladly perform sexual favors.

It was the same tone of voice, slippery and insinuating, that Babe heard now. It held the promise of dishonesty and the guarantee of neediness. And then there was the deep longing and loneliness that had already surfaced.

"I really need to get to work, Eamon. If you can come in to your office, we can sit down for a few minutes and clarify some issues. I want to get your sense of this matter. Can you do that for me?"

"I can be in by 1:30. I'm bogged down here for the time being."

Chapter 27

Later that day Babe went to the theater.

"Babe, I know you need to talk to the cast and crew of *Family Table*. Only two of them are on this new play. I know you want to know if any of them had anything to do with Leo's death, so I called them all and insisted they come in. I think they're all here, except for Robert Evans—you already spoke to him, right?"

"Correct."

"It's hard to believe that this creative bunch had anything to do with it."

"Eamon, I am stumped. Is there anything at all you can think of that might prompt murder?"

They made their way to the back of the stage slowly as Eamon thought.

"Well, there were a couple of incidents that I heard about. I understand that Loren Welch had a real row with Leo. He worked with Leo as a light and sound assistant. It seems he's not comfortable working above the audience on the catwalk where the lights are. It's pretty high up, and it swings a little bit. Well as I heard it, Leo gave him the shits. He started to shake the whole cat walk and taunted Loren."

"Any other fallout from that?"

"You best talk to him."

"Who else?"

"Well, there's Reginald Holts, who played Bernie, the father in *Family Table*, before he quit on opening night. I guess he was Leo's very last victim. Leo taunted and ridiculed him almost to tears just before Leo was killed."

"Okay. Who else?"

"Let's see, there was some kind of fight at a party between Debra Pilek's boyfriend and Leo. I don't know any of the details. They're both here today."

They went back stage and Eamon introduced Babe to the cast and crew. They were a bored and pissed-off looking group, clearly not pleased at being summoned to the theater.

"Listen folks, I have a proposition for you. It will mean some extra cash." Everyone stopped talking.

After asking a few questions, it became clear that their collective experience was that no one had ever been involved with a play that seemed to evoke such extreme dissonance. Arguments broke out and people had left the group. There was even a shoving match in the dressing room. Never was there any peace or joy on the set. Since the start of rehearsals, enmity had never ended. Even now, weeks later, as he listened to the litany of complaints, Babe heard an argument at the back of the group.

"Shut the fuck up, asshole."

"I wanted that locker. Ellen said I could have it when I got here."

"Well it was mine, too fuckin' bad, my lock was on it. You could have used a different one. What are you, a child?"

"I'm the child? Fuck you."

"Hey, wait a minute. Hold up. What's going on?" Babe stopped the escalation.

"Listen, I've got a job to do. I have to find out what happened to Leo Laum, and you all have to help me," Babe continued.

"The play is over. So why aren't you working together and making it easy for each other?" Babe asked.

"It was my locker, and this asshole took it."

"Hey, hey, cut it out," a cast member insisted.

She turned to Babe and spoke.

"I've been here at this theater longer than anyone, six years. I helped build this place. I actually put up those supports," she pointed to the side of the stage.

"I'm dedicated to the shows we put on here. When we did *Family Table,* we had a lot of personal problems. We had two people quit, had a shoving match, a fist fight, and a lot of last minute absences due to sudden illness like stomach ache or head ache."

A member's hand went up and he started to speak.

"The play caused permanent tension. It's as if it was a toxic contagion and the poison got stuck inside us when we worked on it. We all got it. The anger is still with me, and I can't figure out why. Like there was some kind of demon set loose, and it won't let go. If I ever find out who 'Anonymous' is, I think I will sue them for mental distress."

There was a general chorus of agreement from the cast. From the back, the two arguing about their locker continued in loud whispers.

"Please write your phone numbers and emails on this page. If any of you have a sense of who might have had a motive to kill Leo, please let me know privately. Anything you share will be held in confidence."

Babe watched as the cast and crew put their information on the sheet. No one shared anything further.

From the back came one voice: "Fuckin' Leo."

Chapter 28

From the corner of his eyes Babe saw someone scurrying from the stage into the poorly lit wings. He noticed a black leather coat. It was clear this person did not want to be seen.

"Everyone stop," Babe shouted.

All eyes were on him.

"I want you to look around you and tell me if everyone in the cast and crew is here? I need to know right now. Please look around you. Who's missing?"

The grumpy crew looked around.

"Earl Parks."

"Yeah, Parks took off."

"He's the only one."

"Please make sure that he is the only one missing." The group looked about the stage. The stage manager spoke up.

"He's the only one, Earl Parks."

"Anyone know why he would run away?" Babe asked.

"He's kind of a loner," someone volunteered.

"All right, then, thanks for your help. I might call on you to ask questions. Please make yourself available. Thank you all." Babe was done.

Earl Parks, we need to talk.

Chapter 29

After a gloomy evening waiting by the phone for no calls, Babe sat and noodled at the piano. He played a few bars of Benny Golson's, "Hassan's dream," and hoped to dissolve into it, but that never happened. He was trying, too. He stopped and picked up a book about the history of sandwiches. He couldn't focus on it. He was distracted. It was time to get the hell out of the house. He had had enough. He needed to celebrate. He thought about calling Terri, but changed his mind. He didn't want to be a burden and at this moment he would lean too heavily. He had to withstand his feelings and persevere through the strange, sullen mood that was upon him.

Maybe I caught the Family Table plague the cast spoke of?

He stood at the door and zipped up his jacket. He felt tears well up. He had a strong feeling come over him. He knew it as the same feeling he had when he lost his mom. Loss was visiting him again.

Maybe just a long walk, I wish I smoked cigarettes.

He put on a small cap. He could hear his mother telling him it was chilly out and that he should keep warm. Melancholy wrenched at his throat and chest. He quickly stepped out the door and locked it. He turned and began walking. He needed time to process.

After a few blocks, Babe settled into thinking about the murder. He had nothing. Over the next hour, he explored every possibility. He brought a small, folded paper and a pen in his breast pocket. It served as his office. He thought about Ellen. She's paying for the investigation. She seems to have loved Leo. Or was that just a show? It would be an act of genius to hide behind the investigation she instigated. How could it be her? Was she hiding in plain sight? She would be the last person anyone would suspect. Did she have motive? Maybe she hated the kid.

What about Reginald Holts, Leo's last victim, tormented just hours before Leo was killed? A crime of hot rage?

What about Eamon? He didn't seem the type. What was the type? Is there really such a thing? Anyone can commit murder, can't they? Distanced behind the wheel of a car, anonymously guiding thousands of pounds of metal in the dark, it might be easy to do. How many hit and runs are there per day all over the country? Was it deliberate? Was Leo singled out?

Babe had run out of melancholy. His mind was perking like a coffee pot. He doubted that he would be able to sleep tonight. He stopped at the Pierogi King on Willamette St. and ordered a potato/sauerkraut pierogi and a beer. It was fried crisp, and he relished the texture. He sat at an outside table, despite the chill, and stared into the parking lot taking notes.

Earl Parks. Who is Earl Parks?

Chapter 30

Babe sat in his Dodge Dart. He looked at his list of possible suspects and decided to pay a surprise visit to Reginald Holt, the *Family Table* actor and the very last person taunted by Leo Laum. Eamon Krieg had mentioned that Reginald worked at Sundance Natural Foods during the day.

As he drove, Babe reviewed what Eamon told him about Reginald: a washed up self-centered actor nursing an injured ego, a brittle personality humiliated in front of the entire cast after opening night, and storming off as Leo jeered. The guy must have been furious, but furious enough to kill?

Babe got out of his car and stood in the busy parking lot in the misty rain. He looked at the door and his heart froze with excitement and apprehension: he could soon be looking into the eyes of a killer.

He thought about a strategy for the interview, a role from a cop show came to mind, Hill Street Blues, a hard-bitten, never smiling detective played by Dennis Franz, the guy the captain sent in to break down a tough suspect in the interview room, the guy who might throw a glass of water or even a sucker punch at a perp.

That will do.

Babe screwed up his face into a suspicious, world weary sneer, stood tall, spread his shoulders wide, and swaggered in with as much menace as he could muster, imagining a badge on his belt, a gun in his shoulder holster and a lead weighted sap in his pocket.

"I'm looking for Reginald Holt," he demanded of the cashier, a friendly looking hippie girl in a multi-colored dress and multiple nose piercings.

A look of fear crossed her face.

She's buying it.

"He's . . . he's in back unloading produce."

Babe turned away without thanking her and made for the back of the store. Nobody was in the back room, so he walked out on the loading dock. A tall, thin man wearing a flannel shirt, jeans and a purple apron was inside an organic produce truck, moving boxes.

"Holt?" Babe barked.

The man froze. Then he turned around and faced Babe.

Babe took up a position in front of the truck. The man would have to flee over him. He bent his legs ready to leap to either side to stop Holt from running.

"Come down here. We need to talk."

"Who are you?"

Babe scrutinized Holt's face looking for a tell, a giveaway twitch, a nod, a nervous glance: something to indicate his guilt. He increased his cop scowl, turned it all the way up.

"I'm here to find out why you ran over Leo Laum."

Holt's mouth dropped open, a look of surprise on his face.

"Are you the police?"

"Private dick, hired by the family, and you're suspect number one, the last person Leo insulted. If you tell me now, I'll do my best to make the DA go easy on you."

A curious look appeared on Holt's face. He didn't look scared.

"I've seen you before. Where?"

"Doesn't matter. We can talk here, or go down to the station."

"Let's go inside."

Inside, Holt sat on a box. He pointed toward another box, but Babe ignored him, and towered over him. Holt stared at Babe. He bit his lower lip.

"Where were you after the play, after Leo taunted you?"

Holt's face immediately became sad. He looked down. He looked like he might cry.

Time to turn up the heat. If I had a glass of water, I'd throw it in his face.

"Come on. You'll feel better when you get it off your chest. Everybody gets angry, makes mistakes."

Holt shook his head slowly, and still looking down, in a very soft voice said: "Leo saved my life."

"What?"

Holt reached into his pocket, took out his car keys and handed them to Babe.

"See that round disc on the keyring?"

"Okay."

"That's my 10-year sobriety chip." Holt had a look of triumph on his face.

"10 years without a drink, and, 10 years avoiding acting. When I stopped acting, I stopped drinking. The theater and show business was my trigger. When I acted, I drank. I couldn't help myself."

He shook his head.

"And it cost me everything: A couple of marriages, my career, my friends and, most of all, my self-respect. Until I realized I had to find a new calling, a new job, a new town. I left New York for Eugene. I've been here at the store ever since."

Babe handed back the key ring.

"Leo saved your life?"

"Yes. He did. See, after 10 years, I knew I could not manage drinking, but I thought I could manage small town theater, stupid me. Leo got me out of that delusion. If I had stayed in that awful play, I would have found a reason to drink. Guaranteed. Leo saved me—not purposefully of course—he was a vicious little shit. That night, driving away from the theater, I wanted nothing else but to go to the nearest bar and see if I could drink every drop of vodka on the shelf."

"And you didn't?"

Holt smiled and stood up.

"Nope, I called my sponsor. Sam met me at my house and stayed up all night with me. I already told the police. Sure, I was furious at Leo. I hated him. But Sam talked me down, and during that night I realized that Leo saved me. In fact, at the end of the night, with the realization that I would never act again, I was planning to thank him personally. You can tell his parents that. It was because he was such an evil little rat bastard that night that he saved me—from myself. And that's why I still carry that little chip."

"Good for you, Reginald."

Babe hugged him. As Babe pushed back, Reginald held Babe at arm's length and looked into his face. He smiled.

"I know you. You're Cookin' with Babe!"

"Guilty as charged." Babe backed off.

"You looked totally different a minute ago. Your face, it looked puffy somehow, but now you look like you. I'm amazed. I thought I was looking at a young J. Edgar Hoover. Great job."

"Thanks for the compliment, and congratulations."

Babe turned and left.

Another one off the list.

Chapter 31

At 2 a.m. Babe woke up. He didn't know why. Over the last few days, his neighbor's dog barked in the middle of the night. At those times he would wake up briefly, hear the bark, and go back to sleep. Tonight was different. He couldn't go back to sleep. He laid in the dark, thinking.

He heard the sound of metal on metal, his garbage pail maybe. He left the light off and got up. He looked through the small window near the front door. To the extreme left, he could make out a form. If he were deeper in the country, he might think it was a bear. He could not make out the outline of it. Was it merely the small maple tree beside the driveway reconfigured by shadow? He considered putting on the porch light as a sign that the resident recognized the presence of some person or animal. Usually if the light went on the person or animal would skitter away.

Babe turned and put on the light. When he looked back he saw the lid of his garbage can lying beside the can. No one was around. He was wide awake now. He put on his pants, jacket and shoes. He went to the front porch and shut off the light. He went to the side door and slid out into the yard. He tip-toed down the steps and watched the yard and listened intently. Not a sound.

Back in the house after two scotches, he crawled into his bed and slept soundly until the phone rang.

"You said I should call you early." It was Lars. It was 6 a.m.

"Lars, not this early. Really, man. Things have been hard lately."

"Okay. I'll call you later."

"No wait. Look up somebody for me. I couldn't find anything on the 'net. Check out Earl Parks."

"Okay, Parks, like Parks and Recreation? No tricky spelling?"

"Nothing tricky, Lars. I'll call you later. Don't call me back. I need to fall out here."

"Later bro."

Chapter 32

Babe crawled back into bed and slept deeply. He dreamed about a car hitting a person repeatedly. It was as if he got stuck in an animated sequence. It felt like it went on for hours. When he woke up he heard the sound of the folks across the street putting in fence posts. The repeated pounding must have been the cause of his dream imagery.

Babe wandered to the shower. He caught a reflection of himself in the mirror. His face looked slightly bloated. His eyes were nearly shut. He was extremely tired. He ran the water and stood under it for a long time. The heat radiated down his back and through his limbs. It felt good. It was a relief not to think for a bit. He didn't want to think about murder or cars hitting people or Leo, or any of the strange actors who imitated life. It's enough to just live.

Halfway through the shower the phone rang.

The fuckin' phone. I'm gonna smash it, I swear if I hear that penetrating bleat one more time I'm going to stamp it to powder.

Babe started to wonder whether he wanted a hot cup of coffee or a scotch and water.

I might not leave the house today. I've had just about enough for a while. I have to shut it down and take a day off. Maybe I'll do some cooking later, open that bottle of Gigondas.

This foul mood was not like him. *Do I have the Family Table contagion? That's ridiculous.*

He stayed in the shower until the water began to cool. He had run all sixty gallons out of the tank and it was time to get out. His whole body was puckered. He picked out a clean pair of light sweat pants and an over shirt and slid his feet into slippers. He padded into the kitchen and poured a scotch and water for himself. He sat on the outside deck and looked out over the valley.

On an impulse, he tossed the scotch and soda off the deck. He put on running shorts and a sweatshirt. The sky began to mist as he jogged down the hill. At the trail along Amazon Creek, he picked up the pace and ran till his mind was filled with nothing but the sound and feeling of his breathing. As he fell into a runner's high, he realized it had been a week since his last run.

A young woman jogging with a pit bull straining against the leash approached from the opposite direction. When they passed, the dog leapt sideways, but Babe was ready. He danced away from the lunging beast, laughing as the woman yanked the leash and scolded the dog. He realized his bad mood had cleared up.

As he walked back up the hill, energized, he thought: Now I'll have that scotch and water.

He stretched out on the chaise lounge on his deck and took a deep sip of single malt with just a tiny bit of water. Lovely. Out on the covered reservoir next to Babe's house, a young woman in a long hippie dress, soaked with Eugene rain, hair and arms swirling everywhere, danced dervish circles, stomping wildly in puddles, as she twirled in ecstatic animal passion across the top of the reservoir. As he followed the hippie woman's crazy rhythms, he thought about the case, or what little case there was. Plenty of motive, plenty of opportunity, but as soon as a prime suspect pops up, it all fades back to square one. Still, Babe felt good. This is not so bad.

The phone rang:

"Hey Charlie, this is Ed Romer."

Oh no.

"Thanks for waiting, Charlie. You are the best. I have the rest of your money."

Babe smiled.

"Donate it to charity, I'm feeling particularly generous."

He hung up.

Chapter 33

Babe's "new/used" phone had three more messages on it, for Charlie Jackson.

Please come on by and take care of my windows. Please call and let me know when you can fix our sidewalk. Hey Charlie, there's a leak in the basement, can you do that kind of repair?

Charlie Jackson could be a company by now. I gotta get another phone. This sucks. And I don't want to even answer the phone today."

Babe shut off the phone and put it on the book shelf.

After another leisurely scotch and water, Babe proceeded to do his warm down exercise routine that was half Kung Fu/tai chi and half funky dance steps. It included stretching and focused breathing. It always gave him a lift and he needed it today. Halfway through it, he heard a weird scraping sound and went to the deck of his house. It overlooked the driveway in the front. The sound was coming from the back. He followed the sound to his yard and looked out the window. There was a man in the yard digging.

"Hey what are you doing?"

The man looked up and waved.

"Just getting the plants in, sir, I'm planting these bulbs early so you get an early bloom."

"Who told you to come here and do this?"

"It was Martin Lewis, sir. He paid me and everything. He said it was a surprise gift and that I should go into the yard and start today."

Babe came downstairs and looked the man in the eyes. He appeared to be an honest hardworking man. His Mexican heritage gave him dark brown eyes and black hair.

"My name is Raul. I was looking for work. I was in the supermarket parking lot selling firewood with my brother when a man came by. He said this planting was a birthday surprise gift."

"What did this man look like?"

"He was just an average man, sir. He was a little taller than me. He had brown hair and a mustache. He wore sunglasses and he was very happy and smiling. He gave me sixty dollars. I bought these bulbs to plant in your yard. Do you want me to stop, sir?"

"No actually, why don't you complete your job. Have you ever seen this man before?"

"No sir. You mean, you don't know Martin Lewis?"

"No, Raul. I don't know him."

"So I will put the blue ones near that border and these red ones near the rocks." He pointed and explained. Babe was not focusing on his descriptions.

"Raul, put them where you think they would look best. I'm going inside. Call up to me when you are done."

"Hey wait. I know you. You're the guy on TV, in the kitchen. My wife watches your show. I saw you make lasagna. My wife, she's tired of cooking Mexican food all the time. My boys want to eat American stuff, so she's trying new things now. Can I bring her to your house one day to meet you?"

"Sure Raul, sure, bring her by, come to one of the shows if you like, call the station and you can get tickets. I'd love to have you visit. Did this man who hired you drive a car or was he on foot?"

"He had a big brown car parked nearby. I saw him get into it."

"What kind of car was it?"

"Big and brown, sir."

"Okay Raul, thank you."

Chapter 34

Confounded, Babe poured himself consecutive drinks and lay on the couch relaxing. Later that day, long after Raul left, Babe woke up. The sky was dark. A half-filled bottle of Aberlour 12 sat on the coffee table. Dried drool was caked on his unshaven lip. The lights were out in the house. It was night and he had slept all afternoon.

Babe got up slowly. He had a headache. As he made his way into the kitchen, he noticed what looked like a flashlight flicker across the side yard.

"What the fuck!" He moved quickly across the kitchen and slammed his knee into an open drawer. He cried out and clutched it. He saw the light scamper through the yard, apparently making a quick exit.

He turned and went to the front door. He ran down the steps and heard a car take off. The car headlights were off. Dizzy and out of breath, he made it back into the house. He turned on the yard lights and saw nothing and no one. He threw a couple of painkillers down his throat and made it to the bathroom. A hot washcloth on his face and a couple of deep breaths helped immensely.

Babe put on his shoes and went into the yard. He flicked on all the outside lights. He saw no changes until he reached the twenty-foot long rusted metal planter boxes. Emblazoned in fresh spray paint was written:

COOK THIS, MOTHER FUCKER!!!!

It was written in an ornate script. The exclamation points were decorative large chubby shapes filled with color.

Very creative.

Chapter 35

Babe wanted to smoke a cigarette. He hated cigarettes, but this was his first urge. His second urge was for heroin, which he had never tried.

Self-destructive? More Family Table-itis? He wanted out of the situation. His life was under siege. He wanted relief. Babe turned on a few lights inside the house. He checked the doors and windows and took a quick shower. When he got out he called Lars.

"Lars, what did you find on Earl Parks?"

"Nothing."

"What do you mean nothing? Not even an address? He lives in Eugene."

"It must be an alias. He's not on the books anywhere, and you don't want to know where I looked. Assume I looked everywhere. There are a lot of Earl Parks, but none of them are under 73, on this coast. There are a few children in Delaware and Queens with that name but no one in their late twenties, thirties."

"Well, I have to go back and find out who hangs out with him."

"Unless he's a spook, Babe. Then you'll never find out."

"A spook? You mean a government operative?"

"Someone the government will not say works for them. I can't imagine what such a person would be doing in Eugene, unless it has to do with terrorist cells."

"Oh, shit. And by the way Lars, you know someone who can wire my house with cameras? Small ones? With a monitor inside? Someone's been fucking with me and I want it to end."

"I got a guy who can do that. It's gonna cost you though. He's pretty busy this time of year; it could take a week or so for him to get to you. I'll give him a call. He's got some cool stuff."

"Give him a call. Please. And thanks, Lars."

Babe hung up and put the phone down. It rang. Thinking it might be the person who has been harassing him, Babe grabbed it before the second ring.

"Hello?"

"Yeah Charlie, look it's Ed Best over on 23rd, you know, the blue house? Well that squirrel came back in the attic. He's making a real mess. It was five years ago you closed it all off, but now he's back. Can you give me a hand with this?"

"Look you got the wrong number. They gave me Charlie's number. I don't know where he lives but maybe you should go visit him and get his phone number, okay?"

"So this isn't Charlie Jackson, the guy with the big van? I don't know what I'm gonna do."

"Sorry."

"Oh darn. Tell you what: how about if you come over and take care of the squirrel?"

"I'm getting off the phone. Good luck with the squirrel."

Chapter 36

Babe had turned his phone back on in the hopes that someone other than a disgruntled Charlie Jackson client would call. It rang while he was assembling some old winter clothes for donation to St. Vincent de Paul.

"Babe? It's Ellen. Any progress? Any suspects? Anything?"

"I've eliminated most suspects, Ellen. They don't fit into the time line, or they have alibis. The good thing is that the number of suspects is diminishing," he said in a professional tone. He wanted her to feel that she was in capable hands, that he was being exceedingly thorough.

"Poor little Leo, he was just being his mischievous self. I'll bet it angered someone Babe. I'll bet this was some kind of revenge killing."

"I'm working that angle, Ellen. I checked out Reginald Holt, the actor. Leo tormented him the night he was killed. Reginald didn't do it. Do you know anyone who might've wanted him gone?"

"Of course not, who would kill my little Leo."

Jeez!

"Well Ellen, I am finding that he antagonized a lot of people. He aggressively went after their weak spots. I hate to say this to someone so near to him, but Leo seemed to be asking for it, every prank, every dig, every name-calling, Leo got closer and closer to promoting his own demise." Babe was proud of that phrase. It sounded theatrical, sinister.

"I thought that this investigation would give me some closure, that I would find it soothing and comforting. I imagined you coming to my house with some clear finding about his death. You would explain it, I would sob, and you would put your arms around me and pull me close to you and comfort me." Babe could hear her sobbing.

I think she's been working at the theater too long. Or maybe it was a lasting effect from Family Table.

"You can't let this get to you Ellen," said Babe, playing his part in the dramatic role of wise detective advising and calming his client.

"I've got to keep on searching. You'll be the first to know if there's a breakthrough, but until then, please allow me to come by and pick up a check." *Was that too abrupt a transition?* Babe wondered.

"I'll be at my home, if you want to come by. Bring me something; tell me what you are doing to find the murderous bastard who took my little Leo from me."

Were those violins?

"I'll be at your house this afternoon. See you then."

Babe turned and grabbed his jacket, and the bag of used clothes. Though his first impulse was to kill another day on the couch or perhaps in front of the TV, he had stuff to do. He had to find a killer, and, more importantly, he had to pick up a nice fat check. As he got into his car, he imagined going shopping for duck breast and a great bottle of wine. He needed some kind of reward for this constant punishment. He walked swiftly to the car. The cool spring air taunted him. He got in and started it up.

I'll get the check first, then I'll go shopping, stop by St. Vinnies, and then I'll cook a long and glorious late lunch. It will last until dinner. I'll think about working tomorrow.

Babe pointed his car down the hill in front of his house, thinking about the saucing and the side dishes he would include. He considered inviting Terri.

As he approached the end of the first block he applied the brakes to come to a full stop at the stop sign. He couldn't. His foot hit the floorboard without a bit of pressure. His brakes were gone.

Luckily there was no car crossing the intersection. The next block became steeper and his car picked up speed fast. He considered rolling into the curb but the street was loaded with cars and there was no safe spot. The next block was a park. He grabbed the hand brake and pulled up. Nothing.

There was a bus full of kids at the park, first and second graders. They were milling around the area near the swings and basketball court. Babe saw one possibility. His car approached thirty-five miles per hour and if he didn't stop he would be going over forty by the time he crossed the busy main street at the bottom of the hill.

The ball field was coming up fast on his left. Babe swerved behind a parked car and jumped the curb at an angle. He tensed his arms as the car slammed into the chain link fence that surrounded the field. The car slowed and hit the enclosure around home plate. The impact tore off the driver's side front fender and crumpled the hood.

Babe shut the car off and pushed the door open. He made a quick exit and sat down away from the vehicle. His heart pounded and he could feel the blood pulsing in his veins as he checked his limbs. Nothing was broken. His neck was sore and there was a patch of raw skin where his forehead had hit the side window. Hot blood slid down his cheek and he felt dizzy. People started to come toward him from the other end of the park. He leaned over and vomited. His phone rang and he grabbed it.

"Yes?"

"Charlie Jackson, you bastard, I'll see you in court. It's been almost a year. You can run but you can't hide."

Babe dropped the phone and passed out.

Chapter 37

Babe lay in bed. He had been drifting in and out of consciousness. He was at the hospital. Terri stood at the foot of the bed conversing with a tall nurse. When she saw Babe awaken, Terri came to the side of the bed and held his hand.

"You passed out. The cops say your brake lines were cut. What's this mean, Babe?" Her expression was worried.

"I don't know. Strange shit going on around the house the last few days, someone's been banging around the yard, pranking me. Fuck."

He clutched his bandaged head. It was pounding. A sudden thought made him freeze: Leo was pranking him from the grave.

He closed his eyes and had a painkiller-induced vision: Babe was on stage delivering a Shakespearian soliloquy and he heard demonic laughter, heckling his serious monologue. He looked out. The theater was empty except for Leo in dirty old clothes slouching in the fifth row, his feet up on a seat, laughing meanly, intentionally trying to disrupt Babe's speech. Babe's eyes flew open.

Nooooo.

Terri sat down in the chair and leaned in. She touched his brow. It felt good. He relaxed on his pillow and dozed. He didn't know how long he slept. She was still there when he woke up.

"Terri. The skid mark, there was a skid mark when Leo got hit."

"We tested it a long time ago. The rubber particles didn't show any unique profile in the composition. No clues there."

"No no, that's not it. The size of the tire that made the skid . . ." In his delirium, Babe had seen something. In half-sleep, he saw the wet street and the black mark the tire had left.

Terri seized on the brilliant insight.

"Maybe we can figure out what model car uses a tire of that estimated width and perhaps even the weight of the car. It's possible to extrapolate and create some parameters." Terri spoke quickly, scientifically.

She was off in conjecture and notions of possibilities. Babe grabbed her hand hard.

"Please get the measurements and run them through your computers. It may be our only real clue."

"I'm calling the captain now." Her fingers had already dialed the police and she was waiting for them to pick up.

Babe slumped into his pillow and was asleep in seconds.

Chapter 38

Babe woke up as the nurse rocked him gently.

"You can go home today. You have a mild to moderate concussion. You can't drive for a while, and you will have some headaches and feel a bit unsteady on your feet, but you should be just fine in a few days."

"What about scotch? Can I have scotch?"

"I'd give it a few days. And no work for a day or two, you're supposed to rest. If you feel a persistent urge to sleep, contact the doctor immediately. All indications show you will feel better in a few days. Try to stay sitting up as much as you can, okay?"

Babe felt at ease. He could go home and cook. He was finally hungry. It seemed to take hours for the hospital to discharge him. He was wheeled to the front door and expected to find a taxi waiting for him. Instead it was Terri's smiling face. She lifted him into the front seat. His feet dangling like a stringless marionette.

"I think you lost weight."

"I'm hungry, Terri. I want to eat a house."

"Let's go to your house and I'll go pick up something and bring it back. I have some news."

"It can wait."

After a lunch from the closest Chinese restaurant, Babe was on his feet chattering away about crime scene diligence.

"Babe, the skid marks . . . " Babe stopped talking. He had forgotten that he had directed her to measure the skid.

"It's a tire commonly used on the heavier European cars. But usually it points to Mercedes Benz."

"Lars, I got to call Lars." He felt in his pants, no phone. He became agitated and went through coat pockets. At last he saw the hospital bag. There was his phone, quiet.

"Lars. That list of people I gave you on this case, who has a Mercedes? Please get back to me ASAP."

Babe hung up and had to sit down. He wasn't recovered yet. He was tired. It was tiring to walk around the living room too much. He felt weak.

"Lie back, Babe." Terri approached the couch. She pushed him back and lifted his legs. She pulled off his shoes and covered him with the throw that sat beside him. The phone rang.

"If it's for Charlie Jackson, take a message." Babe dozed as Terri answered the call.

Chapter 39

"Are you awake?"

"Barely. This is weird. I feel groggy and tired."

"It's common when you have a concussion. This is how it's gonna go for at least another day. So hang in there, Babe. As long as you're still hungry and have a sense of humor, it's all looking good."

"Are you staying here? In the extra room?"

"No Babe, it's the same day. You slept for about two hours. I know it's disorienting."

"It's weird. I feel like I'm sleepwalking." He sat up on the couch and rubbed his face. He stood and stretched his arms over his head.

"I'm hungry again."

"Me too. Let's eat."

"I think I feel good enough to cook. Let me see what's in the fridge."

Babe walked briskly to the fridge and went through it deftly, smelling and tasting stuff and tossing much of it into the sink.

"We have some amazing pickled limes, some leftover rice from the Chinese restaurant, and some tinned fish. There's onions, cilantro that's a bit brown, and celery that looks wilted but it's still good. I can do something with all that."

"It was Lars on the phone."

"Oh yeah, how is he doing?"

"You called him. Do you remember?"

"Oh, yes, yes, what did he say?"

Terri picked up a sheet of paper and read it.

"He said that Taylor Colgate III, owns a Mercedes, Susie Laum owns one, and the rental car that Tim Hindler specially requested from the Luxury Limited Car Rentals Agency was also a Mercedes."

Babe's mouth hung open.

"Tim Hindler."

Chapter 40

Babe was alone. Terri had left after dinner. He had fallen asleep on the couch and it was 2 a.m. Babe turned on the light and looked over Eamon's list of possible theater suspects. He felt better. Babe strolled to the piano and played the slow, luscious chords of Duke Ellington's "In a Sentimental Mood." He stared out over the city lights. The dazed sleepy feeling was gone. Only a slight headache was left. After a while he got into bed and slept until late morning.

After a slow start over a cappuccino, Babe looked down Eamon's list. He located Loren Welch and made a call.

"Loren here."

"This is Babe Hathaway. I was at the theater the other night. Do you have a chance to meet? I have a few questions about Leo."

"I have work in about two hours, so you're in luck. If you come by, you can watch me eat."

"How about I pick you up and take you to breakfast?"

"That's even better."

As soon as Babe got off the phone he realized he had no car. His was totaled. He called his insurance rep and was quickly referred to a local rental agent who had a car ready for him.

"Can you deliver it to my house?"

"We can have it there in a few minutes. It's all part of our service."

Minutes later, Babe got behind the wheel of a tiny box of a subpar car that had been driven hard by uncaring strangers. These things must be built for midgets, he mused, as he bent himself into a pretzel to get behind the wheel. Though the mileage was low, each mile was like the lash of a whip. The car was scarred. It was basically a junker.

Babe, still a bit tender, picked up Loren and drove to Brails Restaurant, where no one would know him.

121

"I'll have the wheat cakes and two eggs over well. And do you have fresh orange juice?"

The waiter leaned over and spoke in hushed tone. "It's not really fresh, to tell you the truth. It's from the box. It's okay though, we just opened it this morning. After a week it gets kind of syrupy, but it's good right now."

"Okay, I'll have an OJ, then, make it a large."

"I'll have the potato pancake with a poached egg and a glass of iced tea."

"It'll be out in a minute. Thank you." He sang and turned.

"Leo Laum. How well did you know him?"

"We worked together for about two years. I saw him at parties. Leo was always making some kind of party or event. He was cruel to me. I was hurt and angry. Truth is, at the time, I hated him."

"What happened?"

"He knew I hated heights. If I had to move around on the lighting catwalk up there, it gave me fits. I broke out in sweats. Leo knew that and he kept asking me to go from one end to the other, always with the sly fuckin' smile. Asshole." Loren shook his head looking down at the table.

"What did you do?"

"I didn't do anything. I told him he needed to stop moving around. If I could sit and just do the lights and the sound, I didn't think about being up near the ceiling. I would forget about the height and just do my job. But he wouldn't let up on me. After I said I had to just sit, he started to rock the walkway, slowly at first. I got nauseous and actually threw up, first time since I was a kid. Luckily I had a tarp up there so it didn't drip down on anyone."

"Then one time, he was glaring at me. He was standing behind the lights and I was sitting on a small attached bench. working the sound. He started rocking that beam. and it was like I was on a kiddie swing. I mean it was really moving. I got dizzy quick. I didn't know what to do. I panicked. I wanted to run off but I was too petrified. I fell to the floor and held on to the catwalk. My head felt like it would burst. And when I turned to

122

look he was staring at me with this cruel look in his eyes. He was a bastard."

"What happened after that?"

The waiter came with a tray, put out the entire breakfast and left.

"Leo told everyone about my fear of heights. Some people laughed, others knew what he was like and just shook their heads. He knew everybody's weakness and played pranks on them. It was part of his shtick. But he was merciless at times, and I hated him for that."

"So what did you do? You must have been very angry."

"I didn't run him over, I don't even own a car. I bike or walk everywhere. Besides, I'm not that kind of a guy. He was an asshole. There are a lot of assholes out there. I told him off. I even tried to find out what I could ridicule him about but I couldn't find anything. He was guarded."

"You sorry he's gone?"

Loren laughed. "Are you asking me if I would bring him back to life if I could?"

"Leo had fun parties and he had a great sense of humor, but he always took it too far. He was cruel."

Loren ate his wheat cakes in silence. He was pensive. Babe had made him think about events he preferred not to think about. The fact that Leo was murdered strained the air.

"I can't imagine who would do this. I mean taking human life is a big deal." Loren said.

He pushed away his unfinished breakfast and wiped his mouth.

"I'm done. I can't eat now."

"You know anyone on the crew who might have done this?"

"I don't think anyone on the crew or in the cast has that kind of mentality."

"I'll take you back to your house."

Babe paid the check and they drove back in silence while Loren checked his smart phone.

"If you think of anything that might be of help, please call me. Here's my card." He had crossed out the old number and written in his new one.

Chapter 41

Debra Pilek was a hot blonde. Her boyfriend Boyd was always hanging around protecting his turf. Such was the insecure, high tension setting that Babe walked into. The small bar was nearly empty. A few devoted winos sat at the counter. It was soundless, punctuated by dry coughs and wheezes. The bar featured keno, a favorite with some of the older war veterans who frequented the place. Today was an infrequent day.

"Is Debra Pilek here?"

"Who are you?"

Boyd stood too close to Babe. He was aggressive and hostile. Babe imperceptibly moved to his side and pointed to the wall.

"The sign over there says that you have Guinness on tap, is that right?"

Babe's repositioning stopped the confrontation. He took Boyd's forward impetus and aggression and redirected it toward an object. It was something he had learned in improv.

"Oh yeah, the beer is very fresh. We sell a lot of it."

"Great. I'd like one of them. Are you the bartender?"

"No, that would be Debra. I'll get her. She's out back."

"Thanks."

Babe straddled a stool as far from the nearest patron as possible, about seven stools away.

"One Guinness coming up."

Her voice was bubbly. Babe understood Boyd's attraction to her. She was pretty and energetic, like a high school cheerleader. She set the beer down and looked at him.

"You're the cooking show guy. You were at the theater the other day."

Boyd saw them talking and started to come toward them. Debra put up her hand and put her finger to her lips and winked. Boyd sunk back into the shadows.

"I'm trying to find out who might have killed Leo. I have to clear everyone who had a beef with him. You were mentioned as someone with a beef."

"It was just an argument. They were having a party and everyone was clowning around. Leo started to lay into me, making fun of me, you know. He said I was like a gymnast or something like that, because I'm a little shorter than most, and muscular. He was calling me a midget. I really didn't care. I thought it was funny. Leo got under people's skin most of the time. But not mine. I just thought he wanted attention, that's why he did all that, you know, like a child. Well, Boyd had a bit to drink and he thought Leo was bothering me, and he stepped in to rescue me and shoved Leo away. It was too much. We were told to leave the party and Boyd was angry. He can be inappropriate sometimes, but nothing really happened. Boyd didn't even know Leo. He saw him at the cast functions, but Boyd's not an actor like me."

An actor like me.

"So you've been acting for a long time?"

"Well I did act in college some, and when they were looking for someone to play a young person, they always chose me, you know because I'm smaller and all that. Well I thought that because there is a young girl in the play that I could get that part and I did."

"So who killed Leo?"

"Gee, I don't know, really. He was kind of a jerk, but he put on some real good parties. I'm sorry he's gone. I really didn't know him too much. I met his folks. They were pretty strange."

"Do you own a car?"

"Boyd has an old Volvo Wagon."

"If you think of anything or any event that could point to someone, please give me a call."

Babe gave her a card and took a long drink of the beer. He got up to leave. Boyd met him at the door.

"Thanks for stopping in."

Chapter 42

Babe regretted agreeing to help Godric Walpole. The baby shoe affair was nothing but an unprofitable imposition. He hung the charm bracelet of baby shoes behind the mirror of his junker insurance car. He gave them a flick with a finger, and they made a pleasant tinkling sound, that reminded him of the first two notes of "Days of Wine and Roses." He decided to grant the baby shoes a temporary stay of execution from the nearest Salvation Army box.

Once he was out on the road, the chilly spring breeze came through the window and the heater blasted on him. He was invigorated. He needed this: a lovely ride through some of Oregon's prettiest country.

He was already familiar with Figlio Estates Winery. He had been there several times for dinners, wine tastings, art events, fund raisers and outdoor music concerts. It was a lovely spot for a grand event. A lot of money had been poured into the place.

He had never spoken to Ernesto Figlio before this morning, but both men knew of each other. Babe had arranged the meeting without disclosing the reason for his visit. Ernesto readily agreed to meet Babe, and gushed that he was a big fan of Babe's show.

Of course Babe already knew this, as Figlio's marketing manager sent sample bottles of his wines to the show regularly. Babe didn't mind promoting local foods and beverages on his program. He welcomed it. The Figlio estate pinot gris was undistinguished and passable, and the award-winning pinot noir was horrible. Babe had heard rumors that Figlio paid dearly for his blue ribbons.

The long driveway up the hill, lined with tall Lombardy poplars, ended at a classical palace fit for a Roman emperor. Statues, columns, fountains and nymphs, all made from pink-hued marble, must have cost a fortune to import. He walked into the grandiose tasting room, a show piece of Renaissance excess mimicking Vegas kitsch. A young woman in a modern peasant's toga stood behind the bar.

"Good morning. I'm sorry but the tasting room doesn't open until eleven," she said.

Babe explained that he had an appointment with Ernesto Figlio. She picked up the phone said a word into the receiver and directed him down the hallway. It was lined with niches, each of which held a piece of modern sculpture.

The winery room was as big as a football field, packed with vats, equipment and wooden casks. A short, hairy, powerfully built bald man with a large nose, wearing a lab coat waved to Babe from across the cavernous room. He put down a flask and jogged over to Babe.

"Ernesto Figlio. I'm a huge fan."

They shook.

"Pretty impressive. I've never been back here, only to the tasting room, or dining room or amphitheater for a few concerts."

"Please, let's move over here."

Figlio pointed toward a marble bar.

"First, we must share a glass of wine."

Please, don't suggest the pinot noir.

Figlio pulled out a bottle with a flourish of his short, hairy arms.

"My finest."

"Oh, the pinot gris?"

Figlio saw a momentary flash of anger.

"No, of course not. This . . . " He opened the bottle " . . . is my prize-winning pinot noir, the flagship of this modest establishment."

Babe winced.

Figlio poured two glasses.

Babe did the swirl and sniff routine. Then he tasted and quickly made a move for a tasting spittoon. Figlio grabbed his arm, stopping him abruptly.

"No, no, no, no, no. A wine this fine is to be savored." He smacked his lips. He took a sip.

"Mmmmm. Try a nice large second taste."

Babe sipped. He swallowed. Still terrible. He gave a fake smile.

Figlio nodded. "Now the next taste will bring out the fruity black cherry and vanilla overtones."

Kill me now.

Figlio held his glass up. "To, Cookin' With Babe."

They took the third taste together. Babe acted like he enjoyed it, but the aftertaste was hardly fruity, more like turpentine and Brussel sprouts.

"That's quite an experience," said Babe, putting his glass down.

"Look. I have to get back to town, and I'm driving.'

"I see."

Figlio took another sip and sighed with pleasure.

"I'm here about my client, Godric Walpole."

Figlio looked confused. "Oh. I thought this might be about featuring Figlio Estates on 'Cookin' with Babe'."

"No. Perhaps on a show later this year. Godric tells me you are harassing him. He suspects you of threatening his life over his sculpture. Is this true?"

Figlio's eyes looked up, then down, while he gritted his teeth slightly.

"Is this true?" Babe demanded.

Figlio's shoulders slumped. He flopped down into an ornate Roman chair. His confidence evaporated. He stared at the ground for a few moments, barely moving.

He began to sob quietly. After a while he regained composure enough to wipe his eyes and blow his nose.

He looked at Babe sorrowfully. "All my life, all I wanted was to be a sculptor, an artist, to create a great work of art someday. And I can't . . . I can't . . . I'm . . . paralyzed . . . when I face the clay."

Babe sat in the other chair.

"But you have an amazing creative outlet with this winery. What's going on?"

"It is the sculpture that feeds my soul. The wine is easy. I have taken every art class, read every book, and yet, I can't sit down and create so much as an ashtray. I suffer from depression because of this. Godric has such talent, such potential, and he squanders it on baby shoes, baby shoes sold to the ignorant and the sentimental. Bah!"

Figlio glared for a moment, and then caught himself. His shoulders slumped again.

"A talent like Godric's comes along seldom. To sell such a gift so short is a waste. He abandons his talent. His capacity for great art tears my heart out, and I am so sorry."

He burst into tears again.

"I'm sorry, Godric, I'm so sorrrrrry."

Babe stood.

"Why don't you just call and tell him you are sorry."

Figlio considered this for a moment, then nodded, tears falling from his face.

"I will. I'm so sorry." He sobbed. "So what if he makes baby shoes? I will call him immediately. He is a beautiful man, a master of clay. It is I who is the . . . failure." It was like watching street opera with its dramatic gestures and chest-pounding excesses of emotion.

"I will find my own way out." Babe took the opportunity to leave quickly. He turned and left through the tasting room eager for fresh air.

The woman in the toga looked up smiling brightly.

"It's after eleven. Would you like to taste our award-winning pinot noir?"

Babe groaned and shook his head. Out in the parking lot, he called Godric, who didn't pick up the phone, so he left a message.

"You don't have to worry or be afraid about Ernesto Figlio anymore. Expect his call. He is truly sorry."

Chapter 43

Hidden beneath a dense blackberry bush, and covered with scratches and punctures, Pat O'Leery was determined to avoid detection at all costs. He had pulled out all stops by adding camouflaged face paint and leaves stuck to his bush hat. He was invisible, even fooling Dr. Ernie's Jack Russell terrier.

From his position at the back of the property, he had a clear view of Dr. Ernie's tiny backyard racetrack. It was identical in every detail to a real racetrack. Through binoculars he watched Dr. Ernie fuss with a miniature horse and cart, wearing a shiny silk jockey outfit in University of Oregon Ducks green and gold colors. Messing with the harness was taking too long for the terrier, which was yapping and leaping straight up and down next to Dr. Ernie.

Both Dr. Ernie and the miniature black and white horse were ignoring the terrier. Pat put the binoculars down and took a look around. His preparation for the job had paid off. Google maps directed him undetected to the back of Dr. Ernie's ten- acre property via a parking lot at Jasper Park outside Springfield. He forged through bush to the property line. Google maps didn't tell him that he had to hack his way through a dense forest of blackberry bushes. It took him hours of painful work.

This time I won't get caught.

Across the field, triangular multi-colored flags fluttered gaily in front of a tiny grandstand near the finish line. Everything was neatly groomed, freshly painted and well cared for. Pat was impressed.

Dr. Ernie, expelled from dentistry, had created a fantasy world in his backyard. He looked happy in his jockey outfit. The little horse stood quietly while he adjusted his jockey hat and climbed into the cart. The Jack Russell terrier leaped in next to him. Dr. Ernie flicked the whip and off they went, the fat little horse galloped around and around the little track. It looked like fun—certainly more fun than lying under a blackberry bush, bleeding from a dozen sharp pokes.

Pat watched Dr. Ernie unhitch the black and white horse, lead it back to the barn, and return with a miniature pinto, which he hitched to the cart and drove. Pat got bored. There was nothing incriminating going on. He crawled backward from his hiding spot, and made his way through the blackberry jungle to the parking lot. He turned on his phone to see if he had enough time for a meal before his AA meeting.

He had three text messages waiting for him, all from Susie Laum, all marked urgent, all with the same phrase: Get over here now.

Chapter 44

"Put your hands on your head. Get down on your knees, and shut up."

Susie pointed to a spot in front of her bed. Pat was miserable and afraid. He got down on his knees. It was the second time he had been in her room. He looked at the frilly bedspread, the tasteful conservative wallpaper, and the pillows piled on the bed, a little girl's room, not in character at all with the black clad dominatrix hovering over him.

Susie went to a closet and brought out a box. A flash of terror overtook Pat when he saw the whips and rubber belts. She rooted around, and pulled out a ball gag with long leather ties. She tossed it at Pat. It hit him in the chest. His hands never left the top of his head.

"Put it in."

Pat put the ball in his mouth.

She picked up a riding crop, and shook it at him.

"Don't make me tie it."

"Uh," Pat said, shaking his head, the ball gag leather thongs drooping down from his mouth like a Fu Manchu mustache.

Susie sat on the bed, flicking the whip against her palm.

"Report to me. What have you found out?"

"Uh un ra . . . an rah ar oo uh ot un roo."

"Remove the gag, you idiot!"

Pat spit it out. He took a deep breath.

"Who do you want me to start with?"

"Everyone. Tell me everything you saw and found out."

Pat told her everything. He told her about Dr. Ernie and his innocent little racetrack. Susie snorted with derision.

He told her about Leo's roommates, Taylor Colgate III and Robert Evans. Robert Evans didn't appear to have much of a social life at all. Each time Pat followed him, he went straight home after school, and rarely went out, unless it was to the Eugene Experimental Theater.

"Robert Evans did do one strange thing. A few days ago, I was in my car down the street. I noticed that when Taylor Colgate left for school, Robert watched him leave from a window. A few minutes later, I heard music—opera music—and I saw Robert in the window dressed like some Italian nobleman from the 1700's. He was gesturing and singing along with a recording. It was so loud I could hear it. Then he sat down at his computer in front of the window, still all dressed up. He didn't look up for a half hour so I left."

"What opera?"

"I have no idea. I guess it was the one in which the man gestures wildly and emotionally, while almost crying as he sings."

"That's any opera, you fool. What else?"

Pat told her that Taylor Colgate had an active social life. In the days Pat followed him, Taylor met on separate occasions with three fashionably dressed, anorexic young women. He appeared to have plenty of money, taking them to dinner and drinks at the most expensive restaurants, and afterward home with him. Pat told Susie about following various members of the cast and crew. Nobody looked like they were hiding anything.

"Did you follow my Aunt Ellen?"

Pat took a deep breath before answering. Yes, he had followed Ellen, and he felt terrible about it. Ellen was Babe's employer, and if Babe found out, or if Ellen found out . . . Babe would never trust him again.

"She is cheating on her husband."

"Oh really?" Susie put the whip down, suddenly very interested.

"She is seeing the director of the Eugene Experimental Theater, Eamon Krieg."

"Ohhhh. Tell me more." She stood and paced back and forth.

Pat told her. He had followed Ellen one day to a motel in the next town. She met Eamon in the parking lot. They embraced and went inside for a couple of hours. Eamon left first.

"Put the ball gag back in, you worm. Hands on your head."

Pat stuffed the ball gag back in his mouth.

"I want you to get right over to Ellen's house, now. Follow her. Stick to her like glue. Go. Now."

Pat stood with the ball gag still in place. She chuckled.

"Give me the gag." She held out her hand. "Now leave."

Pat headed for the door.

"Go out the window. I hear my mother in the house."

When Pat left, Susie picked up her phone and called Ellen. They chatted for a bit. Then Susie got to the point.

"Ellen. I just had this disturbing encounter. I caught Babe's surveillance person watching our house. I went out and confronted the bastard. A real tough guy. Scary. It was ugly. Anyway, I am totally outraged by this invasion of privacy. I thought you should know that you are paying Babe to spy on *our family*. In fact, you should watch out for yourself. I'll bet Babe has this creep watching you too. Don't confront him. I think he's dangerous. Keep your eye out for a beat up old green Toyota sedan, with a real skinny guy in it. He's got short hair, looks like a meth head."

Chapter 45

Babe was at home making himself pasta al Limone and sipping a Hemingway daiquiri when his phone rang: it was Ellen.

The second he answered she started screaming.

"HOW DARE YOU FOLLOW ME?"

"What?" He put down his drink.

"HOW FUCKING DARE YOU!"

"Huh? What are you talking about?"

She didn't answer for a minute. She was breathing rapidly into the phone, furious.

A bit calmer, she said: "I'm looking down the street outside my house right now. I see a green Toyota, a skinny guy hunched behind the wheel. Is this anybody you know?"

"Sounds like Pat O'Leery. He works for me. He's outside your house?"

"Bingo. Now what's going on?"

"Wow. I have no idea what's going on. Ellen, you have to believe me. I have nothing to do with this."

"What's he doing outside my house?"

Babe turned off the burners on his stove. The pasta al Limone could wait.

"Let me call Pat. Hold on Ellen. I'll call you right back. I am as confused as you are."

"Are you at home, Babe?"

"Yes."

"I'm coming over, now. You better have a damn good explanation, or you will be hearing from my lawyer tomorrow."

Babe called Pat.

"What the fuck are you doing outside Ellen's house?"

Pat didn't answer.

"Pat?" Babe asked. Very slowly, in a soft voice, like talking to a naughty child, Babe asked. "What is going on Pat? Why are you outside her house?"

135

Pat told him everything. He told Babe about getting busted by Susie, and how Susie ordered him to report back to her. He told her that Susie ordered Pat to watch Ellen.

Pat told Babe that Ellen was having an affair with Eamon Krieg.

This news caught Babe's attention. Ellen should have disclosed this. Eamon obviously disliked Leo, and was still a potential suspect.

"Cancel all surveillance, Pat. I think we are about to get fired from this god-awful case."

Chapter 46

Ellen arrived with feathers ruffled. She settled down after Babe told her Pat's sorry story of getting busted by Susie.

"Susie set us up," said Babe, handing Ellen a fresh Hemingway daiquiri. "She's trying to drive a wedge between us."

He adjusted the heat on the stove.

"That bitch. Sounds exactly like something she would do." Ellen continued.

"I still can't rule out Eamon Krieg as a suspect. Why didn't you tell me?"

"None of your god-damned business," she shot back.

"Look, you hired me to find a killer, Krieg's on the list of suspects."

"No, he isn't."

"Why not?"

"He was with me. My husband was out of town. Eamon spent the night at my place." She turned with smug insouciance.

"Take him off your list. And if this becomes gossip, my lawyer will be all over you like the plague. My private life has nothing to do with my dear little Leo's death." She looked dramatically out the window, shook her head and downed the drink with a flourish of her wrist.

Babe watched her. He was afraid for a moment she would jump through the glass and down the hill to her death as part of her operatic finale.

Babe's phone rang. It was Lars. As he spoke to Lars, Ellen came toward him. Her firm mature body was now beside him. She exuded warmth and an aroma that was at once earthy and floral.

"I finally broke into the maintenance records for Hertz. Tim Hindler's rental car? He only drove 125 miles in that Mercedes. He couldn't have driven down to Eugene. His credit card receipts put him in a hotel in Olympia that night. He's not a suspect."

Babe looked at Ellen.

"One less suspect."

But she didn't seem to care. Her eyes were on him. If he leaned his head down a half inch, they would kiss. He could feel her breath on his lips. He was attracted to her, but something was amiss. This wasn't professional. He felt the tightness in his groin. He wanted her and he was fighting with himself about it. It would be so easy to pull her to the couch and slide his hands up under her long skirt, to lie on top of her and partake of all that she offered him.

Babe executed a move that he used during stage improvisation: right foot back, shift weight into foot, turn torso. In an instant he was well away from her, succinctly and cleanly. She was left with her unsmooched lips lifted.

"So I hope we are getting closer to the killer, Ellen."

Babe's voice was now clean and professional: no more touchy feely, no matter how much he yearned for it.

"Susie is a fruitcake, and I think she's dangerous. She is obviously trying to break up your investigation. I can't see her murdering her brother, but who knows? She's off-kilter and could be capable of anything."

"I'll take another run at her."

Babe realized he had one more task for Pat O'Leery.

He called Pat.

"Babe, I'm so sorry."

"Forget it, Pat. I have some more work for you."

"Oh thank you, thank you, Babe. You won't regret it."

"I need you to find out where Taylor Colgate III parks his Mercedes."

"He has a car? I never saw a car."

"It's out there. Find it."

Chapter 47

With Lars unable to find Earl Parks, Babe's list of suspects held plenty of names. The shadowy figure that had slid behind the scenery and out the rear stage door was half phantom of the opera, half orangutan. Babe tried to recall what he saw: a coat swept across the chest and a dark stocking cap, a rhythmic gait like a large ape.

He stood before Janie and Steven in front of the Student Union building on the University of Oregon Campus. They were two former crewmembers of *Family Table*. After they started talking, it became clear that *Family Table* had had a profound effect upon them. There had never been more sniping and complaining than during the rehearsal period and performances.

"Do you know Earl Parks?"

"He works at the U of O, some kind of night maintenance guy," said Steven, who had told Babe he was a junior in the architecture school.

"I didn't know him. I just worked with him on the play," said Janie, who was texting on her phone non-stop, her thumbs moving at lightning speed. She was cute; her blond hair had light purple highlights. She looked away from her phone. "I have class in 20 minutes. I need coffee."

"Hold on a second. But you knew Earl, Steven?" said Babe.

Janie's phone pinged. She looked at it, chuckled and resumed her warp speed texting

"We had an early beer once," said Steven. "He's kind of quiet, doesn't like to be around people much."

"I went back to his apartment after a beer. He's quite a painter. That's why he does our stage backgrounds for us. He's really good. He had some mountain scenes that could go into a gallery, no question about it."

"So he's an artistic person with a night job, he doesn't like to be around people much, and he does the background painting. Is that the general consensus folks?" Babe said in his announcement voice.

Both heads nodded.

"Any strange behaviors?" Babe asked.

Janie looked up. "I saw him waiting for a bus one day downtown. He looked frightened. I called out to him. I just wanted to wave. When he looked up, he looked scared to death, as if I had a gun and it was a drive-by."

"Anything else?" Babe asked.

"When we had a beer that one night and we were talking about art, he invited me to his apartment to show me his paintings. When we got into his place he got real talkative, he wouldn't stop talking. He was talking about art history and the relevance of hand painted work rather than media based graphics. He was very thoughtful. I didn't expect it coming from him."

"Can you tell me where he lives?"

"Sure, he has a small place above the laundromat on 13th across from Max's. It's on the corner, I forget the cross street."

"Can you point it out to me?" Babe asked.

"I have to get to the library in an hour, so we would have to go now."

Janie walked off, still texting.

Steven led the way to Earl's pad.

"It's the one in the back, up those stairs and at the end of the walkway. I'm going back to campus."

"Thanks for being so helpful."

Babe went up the stairs and knocked. It was dark, but he heard stirring inside.

"Earl? It's Babe Hathaway. I want to talk to you."

"I have to go to work soon." Earl said behind the closed door.

"This will just take up a minute of your time."

"I'm in a hurry. I can't talk."

"Would it help if I gave you a lift to work?"

"Who are you? Whattya want?"

"I'm looking into Leo Laum's death. I'm talking to everyone on the crew to see if they can offer any information."

"I didn't know him much."

140

Trying another tactic, Babe asked," I heard you are quite a painter. I'd love to see what you paint."

The door opened.

"I really have to go" Earl's furtive eyes rambled over Babe's face and out behind him and down the stairs.

Babe thought for a moment that Earl would run past him.

"I only have a minute." Earl stepped aside and turned on the light in the living room. Babe saw that it was filled with paintings and sketches, mostly buildings and nature scapes.

"These are lovely. Really good work, have you been painting long?"

"All my life, I love to draw. I always have a paper and pen with me."

Babe noticed that he rocked gently while he talked. Babe saw Earl's eyes move around the room as if looking for a way to escape.

"What are you working on now?"

"This one." Earl led Babe to an easel and stepped back. It was a work in progress. The subject matter was the stage and audience of the Eugene Experimental Theater from the vantage of an upper back row.

"This is terrific. Do you sell any of them?"

"They're all for sale. You wanna buy one?"

"I just might want to buy one. Tell me Earl, do you own a car?"

"Car? I can barely pay bus fare. I work part time at night and I just get by. The U of O put me on some kind of discount food plan so I can eat at the cafeteria, but I don't like eating around so many people. I go to Max's across the street for a beer and a sandwich sometimes. It's hard when you're like me."

"Have you ever been arrested, Earl?"

"Yeah." He looked down, reminded of the sadness of the event.

"Did you go to jail?"

"Only for a few days, I was in a fight, it got out of hand. The guy shoved me. I didn't know what to do." Earl started to rock while he talked.

141

"The cops came and put the handcuffs on me. I started to cry and the people there laughed at me. I hated it."

"Was that your only arrest?"

"No. I was drawing a picture of a pretty woman in the park. I saw her with her son one day while I was eating my lunch. I started to sketch her, but I didn't get it all, so I came back a couple of times. She had beautiful skin and the way she smiled at her little boy was great. I wanted to capture that, so I came back a few times, doing my studies before I started the painting."

"Did you do anything to her?"

"No I would never do anything to her. I'm not like that. She was playing with her son. After about a week, I was sitting and eating and I had my pad. She showed up and she looked at me. She never looked at me before. She smiled at me. I was surprised. I put down my sandwich and started to draw. Then a cop grabbed me from behind the bench. He pushed me to the ground and my face was against the sidewalk. He handcuffed me and pulled me up. My sketch pad was under the bench by then. I looked over and the woman and her little boy were walking away with a cop. She looked back at me, angry."

"Were you arrested?"

"I was charged with stalking. I was in jail for a day, when one of the cops came in with my drawing pad. He asked me if I did the drawings of the woman and I said yes. He said they were really good. About an hour after that, they just let me go."

"Earl, how come we can't find your name anywhere?"

"It's a fake name. I had to be free, so I found this guy who made me a new identity. I have it all now, a birth certificate and a passport. It was expensive; it took me a long time to save up. You're not a cop, why are you so interested?"

"I'm trying to find out who killed Leo? Did you know him well?"

"Leo, he wasn't nice to people. He tried to make them laugh all the time. No one should laugh all the time. It's not natural. I have a drawing of him."

Earl walked over to the corner and pulled out a portrait in charcoal that captured an angry and mischievous look in Leo's eyes, but deeper than that there was a disconnected sadness. It was a terrific character study.

"Is that one for sale?"

"No, but you can have it. Maybe you can give it to his family. Leo was a hard worker, but he was cruel. We had drinks with the crew, and I drew him. He wanted to be famous. He told me about getting paid to heckle comics in Portland. It must have been devastating. I was afraid of becoming his target. He had a killer instinct for weakness. His sister was with us. She's way stranger than I am."

"Do you know who might have wanted to kill him?"

"I don't know. I don't hang around too much at the theater. They invited me to the parties, but I don't like crowds, too jarring. You know what I mean?"

"I know exactly what you mean, Earl."

Babe turned and left with the small portrait of Leo in hand.

"Hey, you said you could give me a ride. I'm gonna be late if you don't drive me."

"Oh sure, I forgot. C'mon."

Babe drove Earl to work and drove home.

He's not the killer, no way, and no car.

Chapter 48

Babe folded himself into his insurance-provided junker car. He would never take it onto the highway. It felt like a deathtrap. He could barely get into it. *If I'm in an accident they will have to pry me out with a can opener.* Babe had put in a word to a local car dealer to see if he could find another vintage convertible for him, preferably a vintage Dodge Dart from the sixties. For now the junker was it.

He thought about calling the Laum family to make an appointment to visit. Maybe he would just let them know he was on the way. The element of surprise was part of their style: sudden razor sharp attacks and relentless bullying. He had to find out whether Susie had done the deed. Was she capable? Did she have a motive? Does she have an alibi? One thing Babe did know was that Susie had the car, a late model Benz coupe. The tires would match the size of the tire print.

Babe stood on the concrete stoop at the Laum's house. He rang the bell. It was a lavish ring that went through the entire melody of an English ballad he recognized as a mainstay of early vaudeville. It was nearly 30 seconds long. He hoped he would not have to ring again.

The door flew open. Susie stood there. If Babe didn't know any better he would think he had interrupted her from deep coition. Susie's intensity was set on high at all times. Babe wondered if she ever relaxed.

"Hey, come in, have dinner with us, we're just sitting down." Calls from behind her, welcomed and jeered.

"Who is it?"

"We're eating."

"Invite him in or send him away. Now!"

"C'mon Susie, it's getting cold."

"Shut the door."

It sounded like a chorus was responding to Babe's presence.

"It's Babe, he's staying for dinner." She grabbed Babe's forearm and led him to the table.

"It's so kind of you to invite me in and . . . "

"Sit down, it's gonna get cold."

"Dory, get him a setting. Don't keep the man waiting. And you neither, Susie." Mr. Laum's sexual innuendo was over the top. His face contorted, his eyebrows lifted and he licked his fat sensual lips as he leered at his daughter.

"Dad, Babe's gonna sit next to me!" She ogled back at her dad. She was taking care of business by keeping Babe close to her. Susie brought a setting and plopped down next to Babe. Her thigh was against his. Babe noticed it was warm and strong. She smelled good.

"Dory, fill up his plate for God's sake. Do we have to wait all day to eat?" Peter Laum's mouth was in a perpetual sneer as if he smelled something foul. Dory dutifully lifted Babe's plate and served him. It was meatloaf with thick, almost chewy gravy.

"This gravy is really 'A La'." This was Dory's way of referring to something French, which meant that it was special and high class and of course delicious.

"Okay, okay, let's get a move on, I don't have all day, we gotta eat again pretty soon, ya know. I gotta have some appetite for that meal too. Let's start already huh?"

"Honey, Babe just got here. Let's give him a chance to settle in."

"Don't tell me what to do, pork chop, I make the rules. I'm starting now." Mr. Laum sneered and picked up his fork. He slid a large mound of mashed potatoes in. Babe watched his saliva glistening tongue clear away the white mush from his lips as if it were snow on a windshield.

Mr. Laum began to build a tempo, spoon after spoon. The sweep of his wet tongue, followed by a short look around the room developed into a rhythm. The food disappeared from his plate rapidly. His pig-like grunting sound was part appreciation and part gasp for air. Before Babe had picked up his fork, Peter was reaching for seconds.

The meatloaf was the size of a medium roast turkey. It could easily feed twelve with the addition of some side dishes. Besides mashed potatoes, there was a vegetable medley that reminded Babe of the worst of his high school cafeteria days. It was over-boiled green beans with diced carrots and baby white onions.

The portion of meatloaf he was given was the size of his shoe, and about as tough. He knew he could never eat it and began planning how he would disguise his revulsion. The smell was overwhelming. It was pleasantly oniony, but underneath was an aroma that Babe could not identify. He knew he had smelled it before but he didn't know where or when. It was a bit like the smell of a new garbage bag, the sharp plastic smell, mixed with a cafeteria smell that brought back memories, memories of giant "number 10" cans, hair-netted women in white, kindly, and overworked, suffering from lumbar pain and sad family lives.

"Eat," Dory insisted from across the table.

"Oh sure, thanks." Babe responded, ever gracious.

He cut a tiny slice of the meatloaf and slid it into his mouth. It had a good texture, if you liked chewing on pre-softened suede leather. He bit into it and tasted unsoftened freeze- dried red sweet peppers. At first he thought it might be a small rock. He isolated it with his tongue and pressed it against his palate. It was definitely food because it slowly softened as it moistened. He took another bite under the watchful cow-like eyes of Mr. Laum. Actually, Babe couldn't tell whether Mr. Laum was watching him or if his eyes were merely resting on him as Laum continued his hypnotic rhythmic eating.

Babe's strategy was to break apart the meat into very small pieces and hide it under the white mountain of potatoes. He swallowed the first bite and went on to another. All eyes were on him. He had to change the direction.

"Do you have any wine?"

"Whattya think this is a store, a bar?" Peter came out of his trance and stared bullets at Babe. He nodded to Dory.

"Get him wine, Dory. And while you're up, grab that ketchup for me. This needs something."

Peter Laum reached for a second or third helping. Babe had lost track. While they were distracted with his request for wine, he managed to secure a full quarter of his food under the potatoes. He wiped his lips and spit a large mouthful of meatloaf into it. As he brought it to his lap he let the meat fall to the floor between his legs. He figured that was the best way of disposing of the final amount.

Dory came back from the kitchen with a full pint tumbler and a bottle of Manischewitz wine, the sweetest and most undrinkable wine in the world.

"I put some ice in it for you. I think it's better that way, more delicious."

Always ready to please, Dory's smile was frozen.

"So why did you come by?" Susie asked, loudly.

"I really had to speak with you."

"Nice, about what?"

"Well it's a bit of a private matter, I guess,"

"I see." She moved her leg against his and slid her buttocks closer so that she was touching him.

"We can talk later." Susie said.

"Maybe we can go out for a drink after dinner?"

"That sounds really good to me." Her eyes lit up.

Peter rubbed his greasy lips and grinned.

"Now you see, you come over here, you get a meal *and* you get serviced. I heard she's good. People told Leo that." His flabby face glared in a strange humorless grimace.

"Peter, that's rude, Babe doesn't need to know our family history. He's got his own problems." Dory said.

"Maybe you and I should have a talk in the kitchen before dessert. We have a few minutes to "pop" into the kitchen." With that cruel insinuating pronouncement, Peter stood and grabbed his wife's collar. Dory put down her fork and patted her mouth dry.

"Excuse us." Dory stood and left the room, pulled by her collar. Her face had a mixture of terror and desire.

"We'll bring back dessert." Peter announced as he left with Dory in his grasp. As the swinging door slowly closed Babe heard part of a conversation he didn't want to hear:

"Sit in the low chair, now here you go." The closing door stopped Babe from hearing their conversation. Babe was disgusted. He was about to ask Susie about her car, when he felt her hand on his groin. He jolted back.

"It's time for us to play a little, don't you think?" asked Susie.

"I think you've made some assumptions, Susie. I'm here on business."

"This is business, Babe." She turned on him and kissed him on the lips. He felt her heat. He felt the tightness in his pants building. He heard his thoughts: why not let go and have some fun, she's not *my* client. He liked her smell, especially because it was stronger than the smell of the meatloaf.

Suddenly he heard a long, loud painful-sounding animal groan from the kitchen, like a bull moose having a heart attack.

"What the hell was that?"

"Oh, just Dad. He will be in in a minute with dessert."

Babe was not ready to have *that* dessert.

"Why don't you meet me at Max's at 9:30?"

"I'll be there."

"Tell your folks, thanks for the meal."

Babe left quickly. It was raining; he pulled up his collar. He didn't want to see the Laums ever again.

Chapter 49

Babe retreated to his dark house to play piano. He needed solitude to cleanse the toxicity of the Laums. Jazz standards were his choice of therapy. His piano was at an angle to the large front window. He could look out and see a wide, restful expanse. He could disconnect from the world. He played and thought about his parents. As he did, he forgot about the case. He thought about how his life had been going nowhere. Typically during these moody moments, he reached despair, at which point his sense of humor would kick in. It was his salvation.

Tonight he mused about the possibility that he, himself, could have committed the murder. Wasn't it possible, he thought, that he could have put larger tires on his car and deliberately killed Leo, brutally crushing him? Not really funny, but it took his mind away from his own life. He watched idly as the neighbor walked his dog. He tinkled out the song dreamily and got up. He had to stop his train of thought. He was disappearing.

Babe crossed the living room and entered his kitchen. He flicked on several lights and opened his fridge: a pre-Susie-meeting-cocktail was in order. He spotted a jar of fresh pear juice and made a pear sidecar.

He paced his rooms, flicking on lights and sipping. He moved dance-like, light on his feet, swinging his free arm. This case was going nowhere. It had become his life, and it was suffocating him. Everything he did was tainted by Leo and the Laums. No, it wasn't a singing group, he chortled. He had searched everywhere. He looked at the online profile of all the cast and crew of the show. There was not a glimmer of suspicion among them. He had followed every lead possible. He had put O'Leery through his paces and sent him through blackberry brambles to spy on an eccentric dentist/therapist. He reviewed everyone: Eamon, Ellen, Susie, the roommates, Dr. Ernie. He even imagined Mr. Laum brutally killing his own son.

Haven't I done everything I possibly could? Maybe I should stick to cooking and playing the piano. It's tangible, it's satisfying.

He sipped his drink eagerly, it was almost finished. It was luscious. He could imagine himself staying home and making one cocktail after the next and wandering about the overly large house. He glanced at the clock and knew he needed to leave. He had to get a table at the back for privacy.

Chapter 50

Max's was dark. Babe needed the dark. He didn't know what to say to Susie, but he needed to find the right character to confront her crazy sexual aggression. He closed his eyes and came up with a scene from an imaginary movie: he could be Cary Grant, playing an art appraiser hired by a super-rich family to appraise some new art at the family's extravagant summer home. Babe tried out his best Cary Grant imitation while he got ready to leave.

Babe needed to find out if Susie did it, if she murdered her annoying brother. Babe wasn't sure. After hearing O'Leery's encounter with Susie, Babe hoped she would behave in public. So Babe wanted it as dark as possible and as far away from public exposure as possible.

Max's was on 13th Avenue in a predominantly student area. Because it had been around for so long, it had old neighborhood regulars who kept the place anchored in normalcy. They hadn't moved into doing body shots or having a scantily clad waitress offering a view of her arse while serving. The decor remained musty, the toilets clean, and the proprietors were old school. They didn't even have a TV.

Babe snuggled close to the wall. He was at the last table. It was near the back door that opens onto a small patio for smokers and summertime intoxication. The pear sidecar warmed his belly and calmed his spirit. He looked at the menu hoping to see a suggestion for his next drink. He wanted another drink before Susie arrived.

"I'll have a cranberry juice with vodka please," he told the waiter.

"You want that up or on the rocks?"

"I want it up, and very, very cold, icy, if you can."

"Sure, I'll be right back."

Max's was in a lull between the after-lunch stragglers and before the pre-dinner and dinner crowd. Babe counted six people. Babe's drink came and he drank it like a thirsty man. Before he could order another drink, Susie appeared at the front door.

All heads turned. All six of them. She was wearing a slinky black number that clung to her like oil. It was provocative. Babe got a lump in his throat and one elsewhere. Babe stood and nodded at her as she approached.

"I'm glad you could meet me tonight."

She took a seat, and everyone in the bar went back to what they had been doing.

"How about a drink?" Babe offered. Trying out his best Cary Grant voice.

"Sure"

Babe motioned for the waiter.

"I'll have a dirty martini, very cold please."

The martini was on the table in seconds or so it seemed to Babe. He was still looking at her hair and smelling her perfume, or was it her skin. She reached across the small table and put her hand on his. Babe could feel the warmth of her. He looked up and their eyes met. It was electric. He felt like a battered eel frying in hot oil. He wanted to lean into her, kiss her and press against her full body.

Remember: Cary Grant: light, humorous and lively, like a tap dancer.

"Let's drink to us," she said.

He pulled his hand away. Babe was instantly out of his reverie.

Us?

Despite his arousal, Babe turned to his bag of stage techniques. He lifted his drink and tapped it against hers. His voice changed to what he came to know as an adversational tone. It was the tone of voice used in advertisements that were meant to sound like real conversations. Most anyone could recognize the insincerity and clarity of that sound. It was very familiar in this era of media bombarded consciousness. For Babe it was a way to create distance without provoking anger. He kept the Cary Grant lilt as he spoke

"I'm pretty sure we will have something to celebrate, once this investigation is over. For now, I have to be vigilant, Susie. I'm sure you can understand that."

"What are you talking about Babe? Don't you want to, you know, hook up?"

"Now, now Susie." He said, maintaining the light patter.

"We can go back to your place, if you like. The night's young." She smiled.

"How long have you had your car?"

"What's that got to do with anything? Six years, why?"

"We found that the tire tread left by the car that hit your brother is likely the same tread as your tires."

"You think I killed Leo?" Shocked.

"Does anyone else drive your car?"

"I never let anyone drive my car." Agitated.

"Where were you that night?"

"I was at a friend's house, an old boyfriend. We don't go out anymore." Incredulous.

"Can you give me his name, I need to contact him?"

"You don't believe me?" Belligerent.

"It's not that Susie." The adversational fluctuation in his voice overtook Cary Grant. It made him sound imperious and exacting. There was no emotional opening through which Susie could connect to him.

"You see Susie, I'm a professional, and I have a task at hand that I really need to complete. This isn't about us. As much as I like to be carefree and drink and dance and do any number of wonderful intoxicated activities, we can't do that—I need to find out where you were on that night. Can you help me out with that, Susie?"

Babe knew he was carrying it off, but he was not sure if Susie would accept his questioning without thinking it was a brush off.

"So you lured me out here just to see if I killed my own brother? You shitbag, you think I did it?" She slammed her full glass against the wall near the table.

"I don't think you did it, Susie." Babe stood. He thought he might have to show dominance by standing; he had the upper hand.

"I just have to be sure." Babe's voice resonated once again, like an insurance salesman closing the deal. Just sign here would be his next words.

"You're the last person I think would have done it." Babe had to think fast before another violent outburst. Though no one in the bar noticed that she had smashed a martini glass against the wall, Babe wanted to prevent more destruction.

Babe changed tactics.

"Look Susie, I just want to get this over with so we can have some fun tonight. This work is getting between us and I can't let that happen. Help me out here, okay?"

Babe's placating and soothing voice worked.

"Well okay, let's get it over with. I was with Tad. We were sleeping. My Dad called on my cell and it woke us both up. It was about four in the morning I think. It was a shock." She said the last few words quietly, slowly.

Susie grabbed her phone, went on line and found the information.

"We can go meet him now. It's just before the show. You can verify my story at the theater."

"He's part of the theater?"

"No he's the founder of a puppet theater: Droll-Odious Puppet Theater. They put on erotic puppet shows. We can go back stage and get this over with."

They hopped in Babe's junker and travelled into the artsy, low rent Whitaker neighborhood. In a small warehouse space behind a brewery, a sign flickered. Susie led them down the side path and up a few steps to the back door. They entered and Susie took his hand. Down a semi-darkened hall, she entered the dressing room. The door swung open and the light inside filled the dark hall.

"Tad?"

A man in dark tights turned.

"Susie, dear Susie, however are you? Is this your new man? Nice to meet you, I'm Tad," he said holding out a limp hand. Shaking it felt like holding a damp glove full of hamburger.

"You look great, honey. If only I had held onto you, oh the friction!!! Are you two going to watch the show? It's a sexy Japanese medieval tale. I didn't write it, but it gave us a chance to allow things to stretch out, if you know what I mean." He spoke rapidly and gestured with his hands. He was smoothly agitated, if that's possible. He was in an artistic reverie, grandiose and animated.

"There are plenty of seats in the front left side. They're reserved for cast members' family. Just sit there, no problem. Enjoy."

A head popped into the doorway.

"Tad, five minutes!"

"Okay, I've got to get ready."

Babe stepped forward.

"One question, were you with Susie on the night Leo was killed?"

"Oh that, yes, it was horrible. We had fallen asleep and the phone rang. It was her father, just awful. I mean Leo was a real asshole but who would want to spend their time killing him? I'm sorry honey."

He leaned forward to Susie and they air kissed on each side of their cheeks.

"Thanks, Tad. Break a leg."

Tad waved as they left.

Chapter 51

In the dark, Babe's mind raced. Susie had an alibi, who else was there? The rich kid is the only one left. He's got a Mercedes. He's next.

He felt a hand on his thigh.

"Now, now Susie," he said in Cary Grant mode and removed her hand. She sniffed derisively, then rested her head on his shoulder.

"That's a good girl."

The dark theater was quiet. There was a good crowd. No guest was seated where they were. It was empty and isolated on their side. No one was around them.

The stage was dark except for one spotlight. Like Japanese puppet theater, the puppets were life-sized and operated by one or two people in dark tights so they could not be seen. It created a haunting illusion that the figures on stage were real. The dialog seemed to be from a traditional drama that Babe did not know. It was a combination of the Tale of Genji and Cat on a Hot Tin Roof. The seductive young woman was flaunting herself at an older land baron. She wanted to garner property and wealth for her and her ne'er do well boyfriend, whom she kept as a secret lover. There was a lot of fondling interspersed with the dialog.

The secondary story portrayed hot relationships between the cook and his helpers in the servant's quarters of the land baron's house. Sexual insertion was shown using carved appliances that reflected the spotlight. The scenes of coitus were accompanied by live music that added a humorous and absurd sense to the piece. Trombones hit deep pulsating notes as the cook sawed in and out of various talkative kitchen assistants. Positions changed as they might in a bad porno movie. Suspense was created by the fear of being discovered.

Babe was bored and disgusted.

At the climax of the play, the land baron spelled it out to the young seductress: she would get the land and the house for her services as his sex slave. If she did not agree, their relationship would be over.

"I am your devoted servant," she cried out. She fell to her knees and pulled out the old man's carved and shiny puppet penis. The music began again, comical and erotic.

Susie bent her head and made a dive for Babe's crotch. Babe jumped. She was digging at his zipper with both hands, having a bit of trouble.

"No no, Susie." He covered his aroused member. He grabbed both her hands.

"Please, let's behave." Cary Grant as a repressed librarian.

Fury filled her eyes. "Behave?" she yelled, oblivious to the play and audience.

The trombone did a wah-wah slide.

She sucker-punched Babe in the solar plexus. He doubled over, and couldn't breathe. He covered his stomach and groin.

What am I doing here?

The music became loud and jaunty.

After a moment she said "Let's go, Babe."

Babe smiled and stood to leave, keeping his hands low, ready for another punch. He wanted nothing more than to be at home looking over the city and playing his piano.

"Susie, come to my house, let me play piano for you. We can have a drink and hang out. If we get tired you can stay the night."

"That sounds romantic, but I just want a stiff dick tonight, and apparently you're not it. Maybe some other time."

"Sure thing," Babe said, relieved to hear he would be alone.

Babe dropped Susie at her car and offered her a perfunctory kiss, which she leaned away from.

As she got out of the car, she turned: "Fuck you, Babe."

"Bye Susie, take care" he answered sweetly.

She glared at him with cruel ferocity, her eyes narrowed and menacing, her fingers curled into claws. She looked ready to dive into the car and scratch Babe's eyes out, but then she just walked away without closing the car door.

I'm free. My piano awaits.

157

He drove home humming the old jazz standard, "I Can't Get Started."

In his darkened living room, he watched the city lights twinkle and played the tune. He felt relieved to be away from Susie. After a double dram of single malt, his mind drifted to the only other set of tires that matched the murder scene. They were on the Mercedes owned by Leo's wealthy roommate.

I'll do that tomorrow, not now.

Babe drifted into another wee dram, and forgot about murder.

Chapter 52

Babe woke early and watched Taylor Colgate III's front door. At 9:15, the tall, entitled son of great wealth strode into the street. His scarf thrown around his neck with inherited panache garnered from fashion magazines and catered parties on the beach. A small attaché in hand, he looked as if he had the world on a leash and it was minding him.

"Excuse me, Taylor, may I have a word with you?" Babe wanted to sound like a British inspector. It felt within keeping to appeal to Colgate's cultivated station as a wealthy scion.

"Oh, hello, Babe. How's the cooking going?"

"Pretty good lately, but I'm here to talk about your car. You see, old chap, I've eliminated everyone involved who might have murdered Leo. Unless the killer was a total stranger, which he may well have been, then I'm sorry to say, tag, you're it, old fellow." Babe the British investigator.

"But we talked about this before. I hardly knew Leo except as a roommate. I really didn't want to associate with him much. We watched TV together sometimes. I went to a party or two at his folks' house, but I really didn't like him much. He was a fun fellow, but he was truly obnoxious. I have better things to do than to spend my time battling through his crap." Colgate was perplexed.

"I said: Tag you're it old chum."

"Do you really think I did this? I went to bed that night and heard about Leo the next day. Robert was here too. We watched TV then went to bed. It was pretty early. We were both beat. I told you that already."

"So then you wouldn't mind if I went over your car to see if we find anything?"

"Go for it. I'll give you the keys, c'mon."

Babe followed him into the house. On a nail inside a downstairs cupboard was a set of keys to the car. Taylor gave them to Babe.

"Are the keys always left there?"

"Yeah, sure, that's where I keep them. I can grab them on the way out, it's easy."

"Are you the only one who drives the car?"

"Well, I do lend it out from time to time. Leo drove it a few times; Robert's free to grab it. I rarely drive it. I like to bike to school or walk; it's not far, the exercise is good, and parking is a real hassle. Besides, it's a waste to use it unless I'm going out to the coast or into the mountains. I like taking a bunch of us out to taste wine."

"So you didn't drive it that night?"

"I don't think I drove it for a few weeks prior to Leo's death. Exams were going on and I had a lot of work to do. It's been sitting there for a long time. That's just the way it is."

"So I have the keys now, and I have your permission to have it checked over."

"Check away, Babe. Have at it. Look I want you to find out who killed Leo too. I don't want to feel unsafe with some questionable character lurking out there. If you think I did this you're crazy. Can I go now? I have class." He said, perturbed.

"Go ahead, go to class. Thanks."

Taylor nodded and walked down the hill.

He didn't do it.

Chapter 53

It could have been the same day repeated. The progress in this case was so slow it hurt. Babe watched as the white-coated team gently pulled the car out of the garage and put special lights under it and inside it. Terri Lemon stood at Babe's side.

"Believe me if there's anything on it these guys will find it. They're the best."

"It's been so long. I can't imagine you can find anything on it."

"You'll be surprised. We once found a few strands of hair in an apartment drain after it had been rented for a year. It turned out to be the victim's hair and the cops indicted and convicted the guy. Don't underestimate this science."

Just then a man approached with a bagged test tube.

"It looks like blood. There's a spatter pattern under the front end. Nothing on the bumper, but underneath it's pretty clear something was hit. Looks like the perp tried to clean it but missed the underside except for the part nearest the bumper. I think we have a good sample."

"Okay, I'll call the cops and have them impound the car. Anything else?"

"There's a few stray hairs in the car. One's blond, one's brown. Could be anything, but we'll go through all of it."

"Good work."

"Duty calls" Terri said. She turned away and dialed the cops. In minutes they were there and the car was gently towed to the impound lot where it would be covered and stored and gone over further.

"Would you let me know what you find?"

"Sure Babe. They'll compare it to Leo's DNA and we should know tomorrow."

Babe left satisfied that progress had been made.

Chapter 54

The opera music blared. Robert stood in full costume and shouted out the Wagnerian parts one by one, quickly switching from a blonde wig to a leather cap. His bearded face stayed the same throughout. As he strode about his large room on the top floor, he noticed something out the window. A splash of bright white passed by quickly and he looked down the slope below the house. At the garage, he saw four white-suited men moving around Taylor's Mercedes.

Robert pulled off his wig and set them on his bed. He stopped the music. He grabbed a small duffel bag and a shoulder bag from the back of his closet. He set them on his bed and selected essential clothing from his closet and chest of drawers. He was packed in minutes.

"Time to go, time to move on, time to go far," he sang quietly.

He pulled on his jacket and a brimmed hat and was out the back door and into the woods behind the house.

Chapter 55

At some point Babe had fallen asleep in his office chair. It rarely happened. It must have been the great relief he felt that the identity of the killer was soon to be resolved. The phone rang and woke him.

"Babe? Terri. We got a match. The blood is clearly Leo's."

"Then it must be Robert. Call the cops."

"I already did. They're going to his house now to arrest him."

"I'm gonna meet them there. Terri, thank you, I owe you a meal. I'm gonna make you some of this ancient stuffed lamb stomach."

"Ha ha, funny guy. I don't know, how about grilled fish?"

"Grilled fish it is. Thank you."

When Babe got to Robert's house, Detective Carenza stood outside talking on his cell phone. He looked up when Babe walked got near.

"Oh, it's you," said Carenza.

I just solved your case, jerk.

"He's gone. We have Taylor Colgate down at the station for questioning, just in case, but it looks like the killer was Evans. He apparently grabbed some clothes and left. So far no one saw him leave. Folks who live in this neighborhood are either students who are in class or folks away at work. There were no neighbors to interview. No one's around."

"Well at least we know who did it."

"Do we? The blood just shows that the car was used in the murder."

"I know it's him. I'm gonna find him."

"Good luck with that."

Chapter 56

Babe called from his car.

"Lars, I want you to give me all you can on Robert Evans. Let me know immediately. We have to move quickly. It looks like he's on the run. He knows we're on to him."

"Alright, I'll get right back to you. This won't take long."

Babe drove around the neighborhood, hoping to catch a glimpse of Evans. He went to the train station and looked at those waiting along the track. A squad car was parked on the street with two officers inside. He went inside and checked the waiting room and the men's room. No one. He drove to the Greyhound station and went inside. It was empty.

"Is it always this empty?"

"Not at all sir, we're normally very busy this time of day. The bus to San Francisco just left and about twenty minutes before that the bus to Portland and Seattle left. We were completely full on both buses sir. Can I get you a ticket?"

"I'm looking for someone. He's a bearded man about average height. See anyone like that?"

"More than half of each bus looks like that. This is Eugene, Oregon. You from around here, sir?"

"Yeah, I live here. Thanks for the information."

Babe left and his cell rang. It was Lars.

"The only Robert Evans in the area died at age eighty-three in Roseburg, Oregon. There are several other people with the same name and two Facebook kids in their teens. Fresh out of Robert Evans's nearby. I went through credit card check and checking account information. Nothing matches. He must have given them a false ID to open the account. There's no back-up information. The well is officially dry. Sorry, Babe."

"So what's next?"

"Well if you have a picture, I might be able to work my way into the Interpol photo database. Otherwise, you can go to the

FBI and get their help with it. They have access to the software. Besides that, I have nothing much to offer except condolences."

"Thanks. I might need your help later."

"Any time, you know my fee, and I'm always hungry."

Babe sat in his rental car in the light rain and escaped into thoughts for creating a cookbook. He daydreamed out of his overwrought mind.

Chapter 57

On the outskirts of Boulder, Colorado, Robert Evans lay on his motel bed, exhausted from his travels. On the run in Eugene, he had hot-wired an old Toyota with California plates and a layer of dust, parked at a student apartment complex. He drove non-stop east, leaving the car unlocked in a Walmart parking lot in East St. Louis. He took a bus back west to Boulder and walked along the highway to this motel.

It was an unpopular, cheap place. Trucks passed all the time creating a din that turned into white noise. He slept fitfully for the first few hours. He pulled out his laptop and explored available courses at the university. He then pulled up his manuscript—almost done, thank you, Leo. Soon it will be time to publish under a pseudonym. But for now, he needed to blend in. He could get into the swing of things in the next few days and be safely off everyone's radar.

He turned on the TV and changed channels. He watched the judge shows that spanned the early morning into the afternoon. He watched the expressions of the conniving defendants, insincere exaggerating plaintiffs, the duplicitous witnesses, the hurt spouses, the earnest judges, and all the displays of youthful folly and societal ignorance, all without sound.

Robert loved it. He could hear a theme building behind the display of facial expressions. It had a Mozart-like brightness that pointed to the absurdity of the human condition and its foibles. He chuckled to himself.

After a shower, Robert stood before the mirror and fashioned a new look. He cut and shaved away his full beard. He took scissors to his hair and carved one side down to a fuzzy crew cut and left the opposite side a bit longer. He shaped the hair on top of his head into a soft peak that ran front to back. Stylish, he thought, as he turned to see himself from the side. Very current for the Boulder scene, he thought. After a bit of hand cream added to stiffen and shine his new hairdo, he walked to campus.

Chapter 58

"Ellen, I think we know who did it?"

"Babe, thanks for calling. Do you need any more money?"

"Thanks for mentioning it, Ellen. I do need another check." Babe thought about the customized 1967 Dodge Dart he had just seen on a local internet page.

"Well, please swing on by the theater and I'll write one out for you as soon as you get here. I just want this nightmare to be over. By the way, I cancelled the dinner party that I wanted you to cater."

Excellent.

"I'll see you soon, Ellen. Thank you."

Babe poured himself another cup of Assam tea and extended his legs onto the couch, twittering his toes inside his wool socks. He tried to imagine his next move.

How do I find a young man that never existed? He must have known we were onto him. If I get the feds involved, they'll just freeze me out of it. And there go my paydays.

Babe called Terri.

"Terri, I just had a thought, what if Robert Evans, who isn't Robert Evans, is someone of interest. What if he's not just a nobody? Could there be any value in collecting his DNA?"

"Possibly. I can meet you at his place and see if we can get a few hair strands or something to test."

"Okay, I'll see you at the house in a couple of hours, will that work?"

"Yes, and then you will make me lunch."

"I will, indeed."

Babe finished his tea and left. In a few minutes he was standing before an elated Ellen at the Theatre. She was smiling and had her checkbook out, which made Babe smile.

"Another few thousand should do it?"

"Yes, Ellen, that should last me another week or so." His bookkeeping was vague and she was happy with that. He never showed her an itemized accounting and he was okay with taking advantage of her good will and extreme wealth.

"I know I can never bring Leo back, but finding his killer would give us all great satisfaction."

Eamon walked through the door. He was disheveled and appeared unwashed. Babe had never seen him look so bad.

"Are you okay, Eamon?"

"I'm exhausted, I'm depressed. I'm so done with it all. In fact, I'm going to burn the original *Family Table* manuscript right now. You want to be part of the ritual?"

Eamon held up a worn manila envelope.

"Sure, let's burn that stinking play."

Babe reached out and grabbed the play. He looked at the post mark and read it: Cape Coral, Florida. It stuck in his mind.

Why do I know Cape Coral, why do I know Cape Coral Florida?

On the deck beside the offices was a birdbath.

"Be gone, you demon play, turn to ash and blow away." Eamon recited as he lit the corner of the envelope. As it started to burn, he set it in the dry birdbath and the manuscript blackened and curled.

"Eamon, go home and clean up. It's over."

Babe turned and left.

Chapter 59

Babe went home and puttered before going to meet Terri at Robert Evans's place. He was sure there would be plenty of DNA samples there. He was finishing an email to the insurance adjuster regarding a form filled out for his totaled car. His phone rang.

"Please, Babe, please you must help me."

"Who is this?"

"It's me."

"Do I know you?"

"Godric! You helped me with Ernesto Figlio. Remember?" *Baby shoes.*

"I remember. How's business, Godric?"

"Oh, it's great. That's the problem."

"Problem? Most people would love to have that problem."

"No. My problem is Ernesto again."

"He's threatening you again? Call the cops."

"No. He's not threatening me. It's worse. It's crazy. He won't leave me alone."

"He's not threatening you?"

"No. Not at all. In fact, just the opposite. He's being super nice to me. Overly nice, all the time. Nonstop."

"That doesn't sound bad."

"At first it was fine. He came to visit. He apologized. I accepted his apology. We spent the afternoon at my studio. I explained what I was trying to accomplish. He was very interested. I offered to help him move into a different sculpture medium for his own work. It was all very friendly. I thought everything was fixed between us.

"So?"

"My sales went up immediately afterwards, tripled from my normal volume. It happened overnight, in fact. I was elated."

"And your problem is?"

"It was Figlio. He bought up my stock!"

"So what? He has plenty of money. What do you care if he wants to own a thousand baby shoes?"

"He set up a website, with online advertisements, and the sales have gone through the roof. Now he wants to finance a factory in China for me. He says I could be a multi-millionaire by the end of the year."

"Congratulations."

"No. I want things to be like before. I don't need a lot of money. I don't want anything to do with a Chinese factory. I just want to be me. Can you talk to him again?"

"Really? I don't remember getting paid last time."

"I thought I paid you. I gave you that string of fine shoes."

"As nice as they are, they don't put groceries on my table, only yours."

"Please? No funds have come in yet."

"$100 flat rate for one visit to Figlio and a follow-up phone call back to you. Or, can't you afford it?"

"That is kind of expensive, don't you think?"

"You called me, not the other way around. I'm not the one having the successful business caused by your so called problem with Figlio, Godric."

"Okay. Go see him for me."

Chapter 60

Robert Evans put his backpack on the chair and stood at the counter. The barista smiled at him. He displayed all the appearances of the culturally hip student. The hoody and cocked hairdo allowed his agitated demeanor to work to his benefit. He fit in perfectly.

"Double cappuccino, please."

"Sure thing." She looked up at him admiringly.

"Aren't you in that new band?"

"Yeah, I'm in the newest one. Gonna have another gig soon." He smiled back at her.

"Cool. What's your name?"

"They call me Trick. You know, like, trick or treat? Bass player. I'll stop by and let you know about the next gig."

He grabbed his cup and sat down. A few students passed by his table and nodded at him. He reached into a pocket of his back pack and found a small baggy full of rings. He slowly put most of them on various fingers and zipped up the pocket. His passport was in the same pocket: Theodore Harmon, Teddy "Trick" Harmon, bass player and cultural hero.

Rockin', this is going to be fun. Good material for the book, too.

He sipped his coffee and studied the clientele. After a few minutes he walked onto campus and found the registration office. An hour later, he was a student, enrolled in elective classes.

"Excuse me, where can I find the roommates board? I need to find a place to live." Trick asked.

The smiling student pointed the way.

"Thanks."

Chapter 61

The search for clues went on. "Terri, look at this, there's hair way down in Robert's shower drain. They each had their own bathroom. I'll bet it's his hair."

"It could be. We have hair from his bed, so that's more likely the sample we'll use. There is no question that it's his hair."

"I'm just trying to help."

"What would help would be a great lunch, Babe. I have an open afternoon. I'm out in the field as far as my superiors know, so let's go to your house and you can cook for me. I'm really hungry."

"It would be my pleasure."

Terri followed him to his house. He put on some piano music in the background. Music always helped him cook. He pulled out a few pans and a tray of marinating chicken thighs. He poured white wine for them both and changed into his slippers.

Babe's phone rang.

"Hey Charlie!" said an enthusiastic man's voice. "Ray Cabino here. I'm getting some rescue chickens from Kauai, you know, the wild ones who are taking over? I want you to build me a little chicken coop. What do you say?"

Babe replied with chicken noises.

"Brrrrraaaaack, braaaaack, buk. Braaaaaack."

The man burst into laughter. "You nut. You kill me Charlie."

"Braaaaccck, braaaack."

"Call me about this, Charlie. Okay?"

"Braaacckk, buk." He hung up.

Terri stared at Babe with a combined look of alarm, confusion and humor.

"What the heck was that about?"

"I think I am becoming Charlie Jackson."

"Who ?"

She shook her head, kicked off her shoes and walked over to the window. She put her arms over her head and stretched, making herself very tall. Her long arms pulled her upward and her heels lifted off the ground. Babe looked at her from the kitchen counter and admired her shiny black hair. She is such a kind, lovely woman, he thought.

Terri strolled to the counter and sat. She sipped wine and watched Babe nimbly work his way through the chicken prep. She was always surprised at how easy it was for him to pull together even the most complex meal. In minutes he had it in the oven.

"Let's sit in the living room while it cooks. There's really nothing more to do for a while."

"Do you think they'll find anything using the hair DNA?"

"I'm sure they have enough to get a reading. The next step is to send it in to the FBI to see if it belongs to someone of interest. That could take a bit, or sometimes they jump on it and we get an answer in a day. We never know how that works."

"And you'll keep me informed?"

"I don't get the results. They go to the local police officer, your good buddy Detective Carenza, in charge of the case."

Babe groaned. "So I have to deal with him then."

"Yeah, I'm afraid so. In fact, you may want to talk to him now and give him a heads up, let him know you want to be able to be informed on behalf of your client."

"I hope he'll be kind enough to help me."

"I've always found him to be grumpy and negligent. He does whatever is easier or less. Maybe you can bring him a short rib sandwich like you made for me way back. I'll bet that would win him over."

"You know, that's a great idea. I haven't made that in a long time. It's so easy to make too. Want to learn?"

"Don't teach me how to make it Babe, I'll gain thirty pounds in a week."

They both chuckled and lifted their glasses.

Later that afternoon, he got a call from Terri informing him that the FBI had the DNA.

Babe went to the store and bought short ribs. He would grease the wheels of the bureaucracy.

Chapter 62

Trick bought himself a throwaway cell phone and made a few calls. He needed to get a place to live before sundown. If not, he would have to face another noisy night at the highway-view motel. He could feel small, itchy welts on his leg, evidence of bed bugs?

"So I saw your notice on the board at the student union. I'm looking for a room."

"Yeah, we can meet up in an hour, if you can make it. We're looking for someone quiet."

"I keep to myself mostly. I love music and play bass, but I listen on headphones so I won't bother anyone."

"What are you studying?"

"Just some music and drama classes right now, I wanna see where that goes and take it from there."

"I know what you mean. I changed my major a couple of times already. Now I'm into global economy and Internet commerce specialties. I think that's the future."

"I guess so. Is your place near campus?"

"It's only a couple of blocks away. You can walk there in a few minutes. It's a great location."

"That sounds super. I'll meet you there in an hour. Thanks."

Trick didn't have much time. The place was fine. It was furnished. The bed was firm and the room was clean. His room was at the back of the house and there was a rear exit just down the hall that he could use to come and go undisturbed at night. The one roommate he met was formal and polite. That was a good sign for Trick, he didn't want to engage.

"It's just what I need, Martin, I'll take it."

"Great, here's some paperwork, just sign on that line and you can give me a check for the deposit and the rent. Then you will be our new roommate. Larry and Claus will be back later, so you'll get to meet them. Larry is easy going and respectful. But, I need to warn you. Claus is kind of difficult. He was raised in the Ukraine. He was a soccer star in High School. He sometimes gets in your face, acts tough, and insulting, especially when he drinks. But he's really okay. It's just an act."

If he gets in my face, I'll take care of him . . . permanently.

"As long as you clean up after yourself, we can have some fun here. We do have a big dinner for all of us on Sunday, if you want to be part of that you can be, and if you don't feel up to it, it's no big deal. Here's the key. I'll just need payment."

"Is cash okay? I just got to town and I don't have my banking set up completely yet."

"Sure, no problem."

Trick counted out the payment in large bills and Martin wrote out a receipt.

"Welcome to your new home. Enjoy it."

They shook hands and Trick went to his room. He dug around in it and realized he needed to buy some sheets and blankets. He put on his laptop and found they had super high speed internet.

I have to get some bedding.

Trick grabbed some cash, put away his backpack and locked the door to his new room. He left through the back door. He studied where the porch lights were and figured out which neighbors could see him. He noticed a door in the fence that led to a back alley. He saw there was a path that went from the back porch around to the front of the house. He followed the path to the front. The sidewalk was full of students.

"Excuse me, is there a place where I can buy bedding nearby?"

He was directed to the University store.

Trick smiled.

Chapter 63

Babe drove up the tree-lined driveway of Figlio Estate quickly, anxious to confront Figlio and get him off Godric Walpole's back.

He had called ahead, so Ernesto Figlio was expecting him. The receptionist led Babe back to the winery. Figlio was wearing a lab coat and sampling wine from oak barrels using a wine thief. Figlio saw Babe, and came right over, beaming.

"Babe! Good to see you. How things have changed since you were here last. Come. Let's sample a new pinot noir."

The thought of another dreadful Figlio estate pinot noir made Babe inwardly retch.

"No thanks, please I'm driving. I just need a couple of minutes."

Figlio looked disappointed, for just a second, but perked up again. He pointed a finger at Babe.

"Okay, but first let me show you my new project." He nodded his head toward a side room. "You will see. I owe you a debt of gratitude."

Babe stayed where he was. Figlio was jubilant. He didn't want to disrupt Figlio's joy.

"Ernesto. I'm here on business."

"Oh?"

"Yeah. Look. I got another complaint from Godric Walpole. He says you are being too nice to him. Crazy eh? Too nice? What's wrong with the guy? But there you have it."

"Pah." Figlio dismissed the news with a sly grin. "Come on back. Let me show you. It's fabulous. This has changed my life. And I owe it to Godric . . . and to you Babe. Follow me."

Babe followed Figlio, who flung open a door.

"Tah dah!"

Babe saw a shipping room filled with boxes.

Figlio walked to a box on a conveyer and opened it. He pulled out a porcelain goblet decorated with grapes, leaves, and the Figlio Estate logo. He held it out to Babe, who took the goblet. It was pretty, and solid.

"Here it is. My artistic block is gone, forever—poof—it is no more."

"This is your work?"

"Not just the goblets. Here, look."

Figlio opened another box and pulled out a clay wine jug, with wicker on the outside.

"I made these jugs, just like from the old country, and the cheese platters, and the miniature replicas of all the statuary on the property. I have an entire catalog. I designed it, I created the pottery."

He held open his arms wide: "I'm an artist in clay again!"

Babe nodded his head.

"This is great. But please Mr. Figlio, please leave Godric alone."

"Oh sure, sure, I didn't realize it was a problem. I was trying to help him. You know, you can't get much of a straight answer from him. I just felt so much gratitude, I wanted to help. Did you know I was going set up a factory in China?"

"Yes, I heard, but Godric just wants to stay small and do his personal art production. So you will stop helping him, right?"

"I wanted to make him super big."

"That's not what he wants." Babe shrugged. "Artists . . . right?"

"I feel a little insulted."

"Now, now. That's how you got into trouble. He's happier being small."

"Okay, I will stop bothering him, as you call it." He shook his head and looked sad for a moment, then began enthusiastically.

"I need to tell you, you were right. You told me my winery was my art. I was miserable as a fine artist, blocked and questioning myself. Then you visited and my hatred and blame disappeared. I felt light and unburdened. The night you left, I had a realization that I was first and foremost a businessman, and that you were right, my business is my art. It changed my outlook. Instantly, I saw opportunities to be both creative and to make money. The ideas flooded out of me. It became easy again. Now I have all sorts of things in the works. So what if it isn't fine art?"

"Good for you, and thank you. I will tell Godric everything is good between you two and that you have agreed to stop increasing his production."

Figlio nodded.

Babe started to leave.

"Wait. Here, take these." Figlio handed Babe a set of four wine goblets.

"Come back anytime, Babe. I owe you. My creativity is flowing like Niagara Falls. And tell Godric, thank you too."

Babe laughed.

Chapter 64

The beef short ribs were searing in the bottom of the pressure cooker. When all sides were done, Babe removed them and added chopped onions to the fat, until caramelized. Then he added a small amount of white vermouth to get the seared tasty flesh off the bottom. He added fish sauce, rice wine vinegar, and chicken stock, a spoon of molasses, chili paste, and ground coriander. Once the stock was completely mixed together, Babe put the ribs into it and covered the pressure cooker. One hour or so later, under high pressure, the flavor of the stock infiltrated the short ribs and cooked them until they were falling off the bone.

Babe allowed the dish to cool a bit. He grabbed a long sandwich roll and chopped some cabbage into a fine slaw with some onion. He pulled short rib meat off the bone and stuffed it into the roll. He added the slaw and wrapped the sub in a sheet of parchment paper. It was a hearty offering.

Terri had called Detective Carenza. She had arranged for Babe to meet up with the police to get the test results. The aroma filled his car as he drove to meet the officer in charge.

The receptionist looked up when he walked in.

"I'm Babe Hathaway; I'm here to see . . . "

"Just go in Mr. Hathaway. He's waiting for you." She pointed through the doors and buzzed the lock open.

"Ah. Babe Hathaway, our local celebrity chef-detective."

"Detective Carenza, I brought something for you." Babe handed over the heavy bag. The aroma was intoxicating. It could raise the dead.

"That smells great. Is this for me?"

"For you only, sir."

"Do you mind if I take a bite of it now?"

"Please, eat as much as you like, that's the idea, it's for you to eat, sir." Babe's politeness and restraint was having a positive effect on the officer.

"Babe, sit, please. I have some interesting results." He opened the bag and began to salivate. He pulled out the sandwich and took a giant bite.

"MMM, this is great. Oh man. I've never tasted a barbeque sandwich this good. And it's got a little bit of heat in it. Wow." The sauce dripped down his forearm and the reddish color stained his cheeks as he tore into it.

"Did you get any results on your DNA test?"

"Oh yeah, we got a match to a suspect in two open cases so far. We never did a cross check with the other information. I don't know why that wasn't done, but it wasn't. Very disappointing to see that kind of poor work out there, but what can you do? This is what we have now."

He continued to devour the food.

"Who is it?"

"Well we don't have a picture yet, but it's a guy from Philadelphia originally named Arthur Dimmick. He was a suspect in a case a few years ago, but he disappeared. Someone else was convicted for the crime. The perp always claimed he didn't do it, but that happens all the time. No one ever did the deed. You know what I mean? No one wants to do the time. Well this guy is doing the time now. They're all innocent."

He shook his head, his lips wet with red sauce. He was more than halfway through the sandwich and on pace to finish it in less than a minute.

"So can we get to see what he looks like?"

"The FBI has the information now. They have the database. I think we'll find out in the next couple of hours."

"Would you let me know when you get a picture?"

"Give me your cell number, I'll send it to you as soon as we get a picture, if there is one." Babe gave him his amended business card.

"Thanks so much for your help Detective. I look forward to hearing from you."

"Hey thanks for the sandwich. I want to know how you made it."

"Sure, it'll be in my next cook book. I'll make sure you get a copy.

Chapter 65

Trick washed his new bedding and set up his bed. He lay down and fell asleep in minutes. When he woke up it was dark and he was very hungry. He had not purchased any food so there was nothing for him to eat in the house. He heard people talking and moving around in the kitchen. He waited for them to finish. He put on his shoes and slipped out the back door. He had to get some food.

Two blocks from his house, was a sports bar, The Golden Grill. It smelled good, so Trick went in. The room was somewhat dark. He sat at the corner of the bar so he could see whoever came in. It also gave him a good view of four of the six televisions that filled the bar. As is typical, four different sports were being broadcast.

With the sound off, the closed captions made the events absurd. He grabbed a menu and ordered the burger with bacon. He sipped a beer and watched the lovely coeds flirt. When the burger came, he ate it quickly and ordered another. Now on his second beer, he glanced up just in time to see a photo of himself on each TV. He was younger and wore a beard. His hair was short and he looked a bit stouter. The word under the photo read: Fugitive.

When the second burger arrived he got it to go. He left the bar quickly and went back to his room. He felt safe.

For now.

Chapter 66

"Babe, I have a picture of this guy. I'll send it to you right now."

"Thank you, Detective."

In seconds the portrait of Robert Evans was in front of him.

"This is our guy, Babe."

"That's Robert Evans. One of the roommates in the house where Colgate lived, where they found the blood on the Mercedes. He's long gone now."

"The feds put the picture out on TV and all over the internet. If anyone sees him, they'll call us. It's going to be shown nationwide on TV. We're gonna catch him, don't worry. Any more sandwiches like that?"

"I wish."

Chapter 67

Trick washed his face and changed his socks. It would be a long night. He took the large stacks of money from his bag and taped it across his chest like a flak jacket. When the sun went down, Trick left the house quickly. He spotted a decent car in the back alley and broke into it. He hot-wired it and drove off within four minutes. He filled the tank and was on the highway in minutes.

He scanned the roads online and figured out the quickest path to Mexico. His plan was to drive to the border and stash the car. He would enter with his valid passport and a small back pack, looking clearly like a day visitor. His plan was to never leave Mexico. His precious manuscript, a book almost finished, was in his laptop and also in a thumb drive in his sock, in case he was mugged and lost the computer.

Thirteen hours later, Trick arrived at the border. He pulled into a gas station to trim his hair into a conservative crew. He purchased some chewing gum and a baseball cap. In fifteen minutes he was sitting in a friendly tourist bar in Ciudad Juarez celebrating his new life with a cold beer. He opened the laptop and scanned the last pages he wrote back in Eugene. He toasted himself and sipped from his glass.

This book is good. Thank you, Leo, for helping me break through my writer's block. Too bad I will need fresh inspiration to finish this.

He smiled to himself and looked around him.

Someone needs to die.

Chapter 68

The living room was dark. The lights of the city were bright and twinkling. Babe sat at the piano and meandered through a bunch of standards under the influence of wine and his own melancholic heart.

He got up and brewed some Turkish coffee using a custom decaf blend he ordered from a local roaster. Back at the piano, he played a slow, lush version of Thelonious Monk's 'Round Midnight.'

The barbaric murder of an obnoxious young man was out of his hands. The FBI was officially on the case. The calls to the hotline were flooding in, from New York to Seattle. It looked like at least one person in prison might now be set free.

The case had come to a dead end. Ellen was happy to know that the identity of the perpetrator was now known and that the FBI was in charge. She knew Babe did all he could to solve the case. She didn't regret spending the thousands of dollars for Babe's help. It was worth it.

Twenty minutes later, Babe fell asleep on his living room couch.

At 4 a.m., he woke from a dream. His heart was racing. He was in an odd position and his neck was slightly stiff. The phrase remained from his dream: *Cape Coral, Florida.* He knew where he had heard it. Leo and Susie's brother Javra lives there. He thought about the play, the chaotic family, the flatulent father. Javra wrote the play! The giant light bulb illuminated his brain.

I have to go there.

Chapter 69

It took several plane changes and a long wait to get a flight to Fort Myers. It was the nearest airport to Leo Laum's brother, Javra. According to Ellen, he had been living in Cape Coral for years. He hardly spoke to his family, limiting his communications to a twice yearly phone call to his mother, Dory—never his father—and an occasional card.

The rental car was waiting when he arrived, and the drive to Javra's house was simple and direct. He passed numerous run down strip malls, and went over a bridge. He was at the house in about twenty minutes.

Babe knocked on the door of the unassuming small green house. It was one of about six different styles that were available to choose from when the development was built back in 1964. The ads for Florida in 1964 were filled with mermaids and lovely bikini-clad women throwing beach balls around. It was America's paradise. Now look at it.

The door opened.

"You must be Babe. Please come in."

Babe shook hands and greeted this serenely calm man. *Could he be a Laum?*

"Let me get you a glass of tea. Make yourself comfortable, I'm just finishing with a client. It'll take another minute or so." He smiled and walked out. Javra returned with a glass of tea, nodded and left.

Babe walked into the living room. It looked out over a large blue pool. Very inviting, he thought. At the side of the pool, he heard Javra murmuring to a client. He saw Javra adjusting the woman's posture as she stood looking forward. She nodded in response to what Javra was doing.

It was a studio designated for yoga/workout/dance. In the room, there were several areas to sit and talk, and small alcoves for private conversation. Babe watched as Javra led the woman out. Someone knocked, just as he let the woman out. A woman in a business suit wanting to engage him in a sales pitch. Javra said goodbye to his client and politely listened to the woman at the door. Babe moved closer to hear her.

"Mr. Javra, it's a universal symbol of the world's abundance and hope for the future. You will be able to sell hundreds of them every month. If you would be so kind as to allow me to install a handsome point of purchase revolving stand, you will understand the profitability as well as the significant spiritual contribution you would be making to your clients and their pro-life beliefs."

"Thanks for approaching me with your new product. It's interesting and different. I've never seen it before." He held the small boxed item in his hand and looked at it. Inside the box was a metal cast fetus with a chain attached. The details were remarkable. The tiny fingers could be seen clearly as could the ears and the closed eyes. There was a peaceful, knowing smile on the face of the figurine.

"I just don't think this would be a good fit for my clients."

"Would you be willing to try it, just to try it for a month?"

By this point Babe had moved close enough to be considered part of the conversation. His quizzical expression, prompted the saleswoman to hand him one. He now held the small box designed to hang on a rack. He looked at the small sculpture on a chain. It was intended to be worn around the neck. The information on the back indicated it was a talisman to inculcate the creative spirit. The small bronze fetus was elegantly and simply portrayed.

Babe read the blurb to himself:

"You are in the presence of "Feto." Feto illuminates the vital path to your future. The spirit of Feto protects you just as you would protect a small child. He is the newborn carrier of the human spirit, forever hopeful. Feto will carry you over the threshold of your everyday existence into the blessed and sacred space of creation. Keep Him close. Wear Him around your neck and you will keep Him close to your heart. Feto's blind love will bring forth your own loving spirit into this world. It is through Him that we learn to cherish the glory we have."

On the front of the box there was a window that showed the amulet inside: its closed eyes and small curled fingers were clearly the work of a craftsman. A statement in bold print read: "His ever hopeful Spirit belongs to us all."

Babe looked at the bottom: "Manufactured for Feto Ministries, Sarasota, Florida. Made in Taiwan."

Babe handed her the box. She reluctantly took it.

"I'm sorry ma'am, it just won't work," said Javra.

"Well then please accept these samples I have given to you both as my personal gift and blessing. Thank you kindly and bless you." She turned and left.

Javra looked at Babe and shrugged: *Florida.* He motioned Babe back into the living room. Babe put the Feto charm in his pocket.

"Javra, I flew 3,000 miles to ask you one question: Did you write *Family Table*?"

Javra paused, and sighed. "Yes, I wrote it many years ago. When I left home, I was a disturbed and angry man. I hated and feared my brother and despised my parents and myself. My suppressed anger had become toxic, overwhelming. When I arrived here, something came over me. I was in a hotel on the beach. I wept and got physically ill. It was a turbulent experience, like a fit of some kind. I was unconscious throughout most of it. Three days later, I woke up and there was a play on the desk. I was serene. I sent the play out to the place where I knew Leo would be working. I knew it was terrible and disturbing, not a play that could really be performed, but I had to put it back into the cauldron from which it came."

"Did you want Leo to see it?"

"I put all of my rage into that play. I suppose I wanted him to see it, but I can't be sure since it was such a confusing time for me. But I know when I was done, all that negativity evaporated."

"*Family Table* was performed, Javra. It disturbed and agitated everyone who attended, everyone who acted in it, everyone who worked on it. The play had a fiendish energy that ate at everyone from the inside. Your brother worked on the play. So did his killer, his roommate. He tormented the people working on the play, and your play may have triggered his killer."

Javra looked shocked. "It never should have been performed. I never would have wanted for it to hurt anyone, not Leo. Oh my God."

Javra looked out at the pool. He stared for a couple of minutes, breathing deeply, collecting his thoughts.

"I'm so sorry about Leo. We never got along. He tortured me. He was relentless." Javra looked at Babe. "Look at this." He pulled up his shirt and turned around. A thin, curving welt ran across his back. "Leo branded me with a red hot coat hanger when I was sleeping. He laughed hysterically while I screamed. I can hear it now." He shuddered.

"I don't feel like part of that family. After I wrote the play, my connection was over, I found peace. I got into therapy."

They sat quietly. Babe told Javra about his career in the performing arts and as a detective, and current events in Eugene. Javra listened politely, but expressed no interest in his home town. He had escaped the Laums and was glad to be gone. After a few minutes they shook hands and said goodbye.

Babe sighed.

I'm done with the Laums.

Chapter 70

Two weeks later, it was the type of warm, sunny morning in May that made the entire town of Eugene kick off its Birkenstocks and throw a Frisbee in the park. Before entering the Eugene Experimental Theater, Eamon Krieg stood on the street and soaked in the beginnings of what felt like an Oregon summer approaching. He felt good as he unlocked the door. As he was about to lock it behind him, the mailman tapped on the door. He was dressed in shorts, whistling happily as he pushed his mail cart into the foyer.

Eamon walked the mail back to his desk. On the way, he looked around. The normal chaos of a new production would soon become Tom Eyen's avant-garde masterpiece, *The White Whore and the Bit Player*, scheduled to begin in three weeks. The set looked like a disorganized construction site.

He opened a large mailing envelope and slid out a thick loose leaf notebook, followed by a letter, and last of all, fluttering down, a check.

He grabbed the check. $95,000! The grant money from December now paid in full. He sat back in his chair and stared at it. He kissed it. He didn't care how many patrons disliked *Family Table*. It was worth performing it in order to keep the doors open.

He picked up the letter from the Fund for new Arts.

"Dear Mr. Krieg:

Here is the remainder of this year's grant award. Congratulations. Our representative reported that *Family Table* was gutsy, thought-provoking, and deeply disturbing— all qualities that push the envelope of the arts and help to create a deeper connection between the community and theater arts in general.

Since you were so courageous to stage a play that
promised to hold so little box office success, and to be so
universally unpopular, our grant committee voted
unanimously to offer you a special opportunity, to stage a
new play, never seen before as part of our new grant
program. I am sending it forthwith . . . "

Eamon picked up the loose leaf notebook and opened to the
front page.

"'Kill Mommy.'" He dropped it as if it were on fire.

"Oh no, must we go there again?"

He picked up the letter again. " . . . The author of 'Kill
Mommy' was Derek Rawlings, the oldest son of the award
granting committee chairwoman. He suffered severe emotional
disorders during his short tragic life. Despite the best treatment
offered, Derek was often homeless or in jail. His mother made it
a personal mission to have Derek's final play staged.

The letter continued. "If you agree to produce this play and
perform it for four showings, the Eugene Experimental Theater
will be entitled to a second grant of $50,000 . . . "

Eamon tossed everything except the check into recycling
box. He walked out to deposit the check, thinking the entire time
about how nice financial stability felt. On his way back, he
imagined paying himself a little extra, taking a vacation to Hawaii
next winter.

Back at the theater, he picked up his phone. He reached
down and pulled the manuscript and letter out of the recycling.
He dialed the number and asked for the committee head.

"Good afternoon, this is Eamon Krieg, Eugene
Experimental Theater. We're delighted to take up your offer and
produce Derek's play, *Kill Mommy*. I will let you know when it is
scheduled. Thank you for the opportunity to serve the greater
theater arts community."

Chapter 71

Babe was on his hands and knees pulling weeds in his artfully designed circular bamboo patch when his phone rang. He wiped his hands on his jeans.

"This is Babe."

"Who?"

"What do you mean who? This is Babe. Babe Hathaway. Who are you? You called me."

A long pause.

"I'm Charlie Jackson."

"You're Charlie Jackson? The Charlie Jackson? I've been cursing you for weeks? There are a lot of unhappy people looking for you."

"How did you get my phone?"

"What do you mean your phone?"

"How could you have my phone number, and not have my phone. My phone was stolen."

"What?"

"Where did you get it?"

Damn you Lars.

"Uh . . . Craigslist."

"Somebody robbed my house, stole lots of tools, jewelry and electronics, and then sold most of my stuff. Then my daughter got very sick and landed in the hospital. She's better now. I'm trying to get my stuff back. Do you know anything about the burglary?"

"I don't know anything. You can have your phone back."

"Yeah, sure . . . "

Damn you Lars.

"I got it on Craigslist. I'm sorry. I'm glad your daughter is better."

"Thanks. She's home. Can you give me the phone today?"

"Sure. Want me to drive it over to you?"

"No, I'll come get it. Hey wait a minute. Did you say your name was Babe Hathaway? You're that cooking guy on TV. I've seen you."